All rights of distribution, including via film, radio, and television, photo-mechanical reproduction, audio storage media, electronic data storage media, and the reprinting of portions of text, are reserved.

The author is responsible for the content and correction.

© 2019 united p.c. publisher

Printed on environmentally friendly, chlorine- and acid-free paper.

www.united-pc-publishing.com

Directions to the Dumpster

By Eddie Campagnola

For my children.

Chapter 1

Another day in Paradise

The sun is rising, the fog is lifting, the beginning of another day here in paradise but it's not paradise for everyone...
Rolling hills of grape vineyards, beautiful ranches, with horses or cows grazing in the pasture. This is Sonoma County and Santa Rosa is the hub for the wine and weed business. There is an enormous amount of money in this region, it's where the Googles come to play in the Russian River and taste the wine at the best wineries in the world. The cost of living is astronomical and many can't afford it and are not enjoying paradise, like the rest. Here in the North Bay of San Francisco, it is impossible to ignore the enormous amount of homeless people on the streets. Every single one of them, has had an individual, unique and personal journey to where they are now. We all enter in the same way, created equal, given no orientation, no hand books or how to guide. We cannot program our GPS for life, there is no map to help us navigate through this experience. Nobody knows why we are here and what we are supposed to do. We all get directions from others to guide us, from the people who are close to us, to where ever that destination might be. Having freedom, liberty and free will to make our choices brings us to the street of our own choice, and since we made the decisions and choices, we own our destinations. When others imposed will, dictates the ownership of our journey, we may not own it but in that case we must still live with it. Every one of us is given different directions, none of us knows what the destination is, and we hope to own the directions and place on Happy Street.

This story is about the directions that led to the streets that have no name. This is a place nobody wants to go to and nobody asks for these directions. The directions to these streets can be tougher to accept and handle than the street itself. No matter who we get them from, no matter how bad they are and how much we protest the wrong turns, we arrive and we have only ourselves to find our way back home. Those that gave these directions are impossible to find at this destination, which will leave you sad, lonely, and searching for new directions. On these streets, most would tell you, they aren't having fun or finding happiness. It's a hard life, none of the comforts of life, most people enjoy, exist out on these streets. The people on these streets are constantly in harm's way, their well-being is not secure and constantly at stake. They are judged, defined, persecuted, punished and misunderstood. They are targets for the label obsessed society we live in, labeled as bad, lazy, drug addicts or mentally ill but that's not always the case. Getting out of the situation is next to impossible without the love and support of family, friends and society, who can give the directions back home, to Happy Street.

Out of the dissipating fog rides a man on a bicycle, his name is Eddie, they call him, "Fast Eddie", on the street. He's been on these streets for five years. Riding his bicycle on the avenue, his headset on, playing, "U2", "Where the Streets have no Name", just like these streets. The music continues in his ears, as he rides fast on his bicycle past the homeless camp the Counties Sheriff Department is closing down, finishing up with the nights work, they are removing the people, its either moving day or jail for them. Left behind are their piles of former life belongings, clothes, pictures, whatever they had in their camp, now a pile of garbage to be gone through by other homeless.

The homeless are the favorite target for police, they are easy and everyone on the street has, at one time or another, been engaged by them. "Fast Eddie' has, so, he moves fast, by them.

Eddie is unique on these streets, to start, he grew up in New Jersey but has traveled the country and spent significant time in several states. Over the last ten years, since his wife passed away, he's been exercising and exploring his free spirit, even exploiting it. Eddie hates labels and would deny he's any that are placed on him. He's a happy go lucky guy, slightly autistic and neurologically impaired, a worry wart, like Atlas, he carries the weight of the world on his shoulders. He prefers to live and let live, and love one another but has strong beliefs and he doesn't shy away from letting them be known, he's an activist for anything he thinks is a righteous and just cause. He stands up for what is right and selflessly puts himself out in the process, which has cost him. He doesn't like to be serious, if he doesn't have to, always trying to make life fun, he maintains a great sense of humor and can definitely be misunderstood. With exceptions, he has some firm beliefs he won't compromise, one of them is authorities. He exercises his rights and they find that he is difficult to prosecute. He's different in a lot of other ways, as well, he doesn't steal, rob or take from anyone or any store, as some out here do, and he's had all his belongings stolen ten times over. He cleans up after himself and never leaves a mess, he encourage others to do the same. He's considered weird by these streets but those that know him, like "Killer Pat", will tell you, "From what I seen and know, out here, on these streets, Fast Eddie's not weird at all. I know him for a few years, and we hung around that internet café and casino. They all think he's weird cuz they see he cleans up after himself. He even keeps his cigarette remains and any candy wrappers in his pocket until he finds a garbage can. He does the right thing, all the time, never fucks anybody and will help you if you need help. Once I saw him carrying some old ladies groceries down the Avenue and up the three story buildings stairs to her door. He gives the police no reason to engage him. I see him work hard, he got several part time jobs. He waves a sign for that mattress store, on the avenue and caters part time. He's a referee, yea, he officiates sports but not as much as he once did. In my opinion, "Fast Eddie" is a righteous brother, once you get to know him."

More homeless waking up in store fronts, by the store keepers, as Eddie flies by on his bicycle, he's got to ride fast, police target bikers with back packs. Other homeless ride by him in the opposite direction, with several large bags of recyclables, they have been collecting overnight, on their backs, as they ride bikes to the recycle center. They can cash in there and pick up free bread and pastries. Others take their position at intersections, pan handling with small signs requesting handouts. Many gather at 600 Morgan Street, Santa Rosa, a homeless services center, operated by Catholic Charities that provides Eddie with a mailing address to receive his mail, they have showers also. They don't actually house anyone there, they have housing at another location. In addition to signing up for services, those seeking shelter must interview and usually wait for a bed. They must check back for an available room at eight am on Mondays and Wednesdays. Eddie has interviewed and signed up for a bed but hasn't gotten one. The homeless service centers clients, a diverse group of people and characters that is represented by all genders, religions and ethnicities. A high percentage have physical ailments, disorders and disabilities. It is difficult to maintain personal hygiene, as stores and restaurants don't allow public use of their rest rooms, to keep the homeless away. This can sometimes make checking in there, uncomfortable for some, it is not a place for those with weak stomachs. When he first became homeless, he would plan to eat before going there, his appetite effected by others unattended personal hygiene. He had a hard time eating at the soup kitchen, for the same reason.

He practiced the same table manners he always had, he didn't care that he was in a soup kitchen and the only patron in the dining room with his napkin folded on his lap and his elbows, never touching the table. The appearance and manners of others was something that over time he would get use to or block out of his mind, eventually, he didn't even think about it at all.

Eddie doesn't judge anyone or even suspect anything, he's nice and kind to everyone, he believes in loving one another, this is taken as a sign of weakness, on the street and he is often victimized, as a result. This is the Wild West and anything goes. He grew up back east, where there are unwritten guidelines among those involved in questionable activities, they have a code. If you are involved, you know what comes with the territory. If you're not taking part in their lifestyle and live clean, they respect you. In the Wild West, it's easy to get stuck in the cross fire of dangerous activities. Just minding your own business, sometimes might not be enough, one can easily be swept into a situation, simply for being in the wrong place at the wrong time. It's hard to be guarded if one is truly nonjudgmental and even more unsuspecting, as Eddie is.

He wonders, every day, how people end up out here. He knows how he did and it's not been his choice or where he wants to be. As for everyone else, they all have a story and most would tell you, they aren't having fun or finding happiness. It's a hard life, none of the comforts of life, most people enjoy, exist out on the streets, their well-being is not secure and constantly at stake. They are judged, defined and misunderstood. They are targets for the rest of society, labeled as bad, lazy, drug addicts or mentally ill but that's not always the case.

In addition to that, there are physical attacks that take place on the street. Goon Squads that attack the homeless and beat up the less fortunate, one has to be constantly on guard. Some drive by in trucks, either throwing eggs or shooting paint guns at the defenseless lower dregs of society. They are cowards, Eddie stands up to them and arms himself with rocks to throw back. A friend of his, told him, "Be careful, they will catch you and beat you up." Eddie suspected less of them and ignored his suggestion. A few nights later, a truck passed him and made a U-turn heading back in his direction. Here was his chance, he reached down and picked up two rocks. As they got close, he turned and raised a rock to throw. The driver panicked and floored the gas pedal. The passenger was armed with a paint gun and he fired up and into the windshield. He had fallen back, as the truck accelerated and yellow paint splattered inside the vehicle. He didn't get off a good throw, being off balance on a bicycle, he almost fell off. He chased them down the street, hopped off the bike and threw but came up short. He had proved his theory, they were cowards. He tries his best to emulate Jesus Christ, he's good but not that good. He sometimes reacts to those that hurt him with unkind words, never actions. Sometimes, he has to defend himself against attackers, he finds it hard to always turn the other check, and he would not survive if he did.

There are many homeless using drugs or what is actually, self-medicating, they are using them because of some other bigger problem. Eddie believes the drugs are a side effect or symptom of that bigger problem. He feels, that's why the success rate for clients is so low in the programs and rehabs, they don't address the problem. Even the small amount of people who stop using drugs, remain addicted, just to something else, like the program itself, religion or work.

Most of the homeless have been directed here, by their families and friends, same as a president gets directed to the White House. Except, instead of leading us with

Presidential learned behavior, these directions are designed with the learned behavior that is for garbage, what Eddie calls, "directions to the dumpster", that come from those that are close to them.

That was his case, learned behavior, he was taught that he was garbage and given "directions to the dumpster". We often hear people receiving accolades or honors for some accomplishment say, "I couldn't have done it without the love and support of my friends and family." or " I don't know where I would be without the love and support of my family.", well, the people on these streets have got a pretty good idea of what that answer could be and they know exactly where they might be without that love and support.

Getting out of this situation is next to impossible, especially with the north bays cost of living and without the necessary love and support from family. Nobody knows you when you're down and out. Many friends and family will manipulate a situation to justify or give them an excuse to no longer know you.

This region is, by far, the most expensive region to live in the country. It's beautiful, paradise, the Googles live here, between them, the wineries and the new weed money, the cost of living cannot be met by a single person, without a skilled labor, degree or trade, and you need a dual income. There is no moderate to low income housing, the money got here so fast, and they have been un-able to keep up with the demand for labor that comes with the service demands of the wealthy. Many who work in the service industry are illegals, who live in small homes with multiple residents. A lot of unskilled, single people like Eddie, with emotionally learned behavior issues, make up the homeless population in addition to the many self-medicating others, with issues that go un-addressed. However, they are all labeled and defined together, as one group and all considered thieves, untrustworthy and lazy.

Unfortunately, society's labels, as well as criminal records for drugs, used by many to escape the emotions or feelings brought on by their environment or upbringing, leads to a life of crime, as they are unsuitable for hiring. This makes many of the generalizations true but like any generalization, that doesn't mean everybody. Eddie has to endure both sides of this, nobody trusts him and his peers steal from him. They steal everything, nothing is sacred and accumulating things with no safe place to keep them, puts those things at risk of being taken and that's exactly what happens. On one occasion, he had a bag stolen which contained his daughter, Christina's baby book. In the book were hand written letters from his daughter's immediate family, her brothers, mom and himself. His wife, Karen, her mom, who passed away when his daughter was four, wrote a heartfelt prognosis of the future she planned on spending with her daughter, it was all he had to give to her and it was beautiful, he looked forward to giving it to her, when he was re-united with her someday, it was stolen. He frantically searched the area, crying his eyes out for three days. He hung up and handed out fliers requesting they return it by dropping it off at the library, no questions asked, it was never found or returned. It was priceless to him, the most valuable possession he had or could have, gone.

None of the public places or private businesses make it easy for the people in the street, they make it harder, no electrical outlets, to charge a phone, no mirrors to make one presentable, nothing to improve yourself.
They want to keep the homeless, homeless, to make fun of, and to have somebody to make themselves feel better about themselves.

Eddie remains undeterred, resolved to do the right thing all the time. He loves one another and shares whatever he has with anybody out here, on the street.

While walking the avenue he looks on the ground and spots a wallet, a quick peek reveals, it's got some $20's in it. He looks for an ID and sure enough it belongs to someone that lives at the welfare hotel on the Avenue. He's hungry and broke but he brings it to the man. It's a housing project for veterans and he's happy to return it. Waiting in the reception area, after announcing who he wished to visit, he thinks about how he could have spent the money but changes his thoughts to how happy the man who owns the wallet will be. The man appears and asks, "Who's here to see me?" Eddie says, "I am and I think I found something of yours." He gives it to the man, turns and begins to walks away but the man calls him back and says, "Hey, thanks a lot, saved me some money for new ID's, Do you need a couple bucks?" Eddie tells him," that's not why I did it but I'm hungry and broke and could use a couple bucks." He literally hands him two dollars, he looks at the bills and says," thank you" and continues on his way. Than the man who got his wallet back says, "Hey, Fast Eddie, they ought to change your name to "The Saint of Santa Rosa Ave".

He's on his way, he will ride to the dollar store and get two $1 food items, then to the mattress store, where he works part time. He has friends there, the Salespeople and especially, the Manager, Glen. He grew up in England and immigrated to the US with his family as a teenager. Glen is married and has two young children. He seems to be more understanding of Eddie's situation than most, maybe because of where he comes from? As an American, Eddie doesn't know how the English behave towards homeless or if it is even an issue, as it is in the US, perhaps he is just a compassionate man. They have similar soccer backgrounds and play ping pong. Eddie does the sign waving for the store and sets up the outdoor display on holiday weekends. He can heat up the food he just bought. He used to be able to leave food here and safely leave his things but Corporate Management found out and stopped him. Glen, still lets him use the microwave and there is a ping pong table, they have a healthy rivalry on. He eats, they play and talk. Eddie tells Glen, "I'm tired of spinning my wheels in the mud. Every time I put some money together, something bad happens or I spend it on a few nights at the motel. When I buy things, they get stolen. The times I've roughed it and held the money, I've lost patience and lost it at the casino or had it stolen. I've shared all the bad experiences I've had with you. Glen, you know there have been some things that have happened to me that are, at the very least, unusual incidents and have been hard for me to overcome. Each incident takes me time to recover from and each time, the incident is worse than the last time." Glen says, "I know but you keep on trying and that's admirable, to say the least. I do know this, you've got to stay away from that casino." Which the casino has taken care of for Eddie and he let Glen know, "They kicked me out and I'm not allowed there anymore." He would go there without money, to get out of the rain or for free water. Sometimes, he would find money on the ground, they got hip to him and threw him out. They claimed because they caught him smoking marijuana and since the casino is considered federal land, owned by Native Americans, marijuana is illegal on their property.

Eddie wins the first game of ping pong. Glen reminds him of his work schedule, "Hey, Eddie, don't forget, it's fourth of July and you are setting up the outdoor display, doing security and sign waving all weekend!" He replies, "I think I'm taking the money and going back east, I need to be near my kids, I miss them terribly, its killing me emotionally." Glen wins the second game. He says, "But will you be able to see them, especially your daughter?" Eddie explains, "I don't care, I just have this feeling that I need to be close to them. It's my home that I need, in my heart, that's where it is and it's where my heart is, with my kids, I need to get back home. I'll see you Friday but before I go, let's play one more." Glen wins the third game and Eddie leaves.

He goes to the back of the store, he thinks of home, where his heart is, with his children. Every day, every moment, he thinks of them, especially his daughter, he cries his eye balls out for her. He has a visual of her being taken away by police, throwing herself at him, while in the policeman's arms and it haunts him daily. He hears other children call their father, "Daddy?!?" and he looks, to see if it's her. He has no money and that means, no self-medication or, in his case, speed, which is what he uses to stop the feelings he gets, the emotions created by the visuals he has in his head and the haunting everyday sounds that bring him to that very sad place. He wonders why bad things happen to good people. He always thought, if he did the right thing, everything will work out right. The things that make him cry uncontrollably, making it impossible for him to function, as he becomes emotionally paralyzed. Meth Amphetamine prevents him from crying and feeling the emotions, he hides away. He usually doesn't sleep, nobody does out on the street, their bodies just turn off, and they pass out. He goes behind the store, next to the dumpster, where his learned behavior from his family and others, has directed him, he has been taught that he is garbage. He can tell his bodies about to shut down. He prays, every time, he's about to sleep, this nightmare will be over when he wakes up. As he's fading out, he remembers what life used to be like for him, before this nightmare began….

Music plays in Eddie's head, all the time, this time, he hears "10,000 Maniacs" "These are Days". "You'll remember. Never before and never since, I promise will the whole world be warm as this. And as you feel it, you'll know it's true that you are blessed and lucky. It's true that you are touched by something that will grow and bloom in you. These are days you'll remember. When May is rushing over you with desire to be a part of the miracles you see in every hour. You'll know, it's true, that you are blessed and lucky. These are days, you might fill will laughter, until you break. These days you might feel a shaft of light make its way across your face and when you do, you'll know how it was meant to be. See the signs and know their meaning. It's true, you'll know how it was meant to be. Hear the signs and know their meaning, they're speaking to you." He passes out…

Chapter 2

Dreaming of the past

He slips into dreamland where he dreams he's home again, before the nightmare began. He dream that he wakes up and tells his wife, Karen, about the horrible nightmare. "Honey, I just had the worst nightmare, I was homeless and". He's interrupted, as their four-year-old daughter, Christina, excited about every new day, jumps on the bed, making her breakfast order, "Daddy, it's time to get up and make breakfast, French toast, please. I will help you!" Eddie kisses his wife, she pulls him back for another and says, "I love you." He says, "I love you too, every time you kiss me it's like the first time." then she slowly makes her way to the bathroom and prepares for her long day at work. Christina and Eddie would gather the pots and pans, not to cook with to wake up her brothers with. They would enter the boy's room, Mike, 14 Derek, 13, my step son's, from Karen's first marriage and Frank, 14, Eddie's son from his first marriage. The father and daughter team enter the adolescent boy cave, for the first alarm, with the pots and pans clanging musical, rhythmic beat, they would each roll over for a snooze, before heading back to the kitchen, Christina would threaten, "We'll be back!" As they headed to the kitchen to make breakfast. Christina, would always decide, she reiterated her favorite, "French toast, Daddy!" She helped him with everything and couldn't wait for her brothers to join them. "I think it's time they get up, Daddy." Back they went, to the boy cave and the second alarm, this time a marching rhythm, more orderly and less abrupt but equally annoying, Christina warns her Daddy, "Be careful Daddy, pillows might fly, you should be ready to duck!" and so he did, "Just missed you Daddy, good ducking". They would never hit their sister, not with a feather, for there would be hell to pay, if they did. She was Daddy's girl, the boys would constantly complain,

"How come she gets whatever she wants?" or "You favor her." Eddie would simply reply, "Yes, of course I do, might as well get used to it because, that's just the way it is. I love you all but she's my girl, you'll understand some day." Frank was first and heard from Christina, "You just missed Daddy by that much." She shows an inch with her index and thumb fingers." He replies, "Good morning, Christina "Bom Beana". Morning dad, you got lucky with the pillow." he was pretty easy and just as Karen was finishing in the bathroom, Eddie directed him, "Morning Buddy, the bathroom is all yours. The Yankees got lucky, last night, thanks to the curse of the Bambino. This morning, Christina had my back, I was warned of the potential attack, everybody needs the bathroom, don't take too long.", he entered, chanting, "1918, 1918". Eddie had to time these things to make sure he limited the amount of unavoidable chaos.

Derek was next to surface, he would visit his Mom first, she was continuing with her morning rituals in the bedroom, Derek was warm and loving and had to have his morning hug with his mom first, then to Christina, he hugged her saying, "Morning Christina, I love you." She said, "I love you too, DD. French toast, coming up." Mike was last to appear, always protesting or explaining why he couldn't go to school, "I can't go to school today, my head, my stomach and I think I have a fever." I would alert Karen, "Honey, Mike is sick again. Mike, honestly, every day? Go see your Mom." She kissed his forehead saying, "No fever but if you don't feel well after your first class, go to the school nurse and have her take your temperature, and I love you."

They all ate and after breakfast, it was off to the various locations and transportation modes, Mommy to the train, the boys to a bus or directly to school. Then, it was just Christina and Eddie. They would have fun, either attending to the massive pile of laundry, dishes or another type of house work. After that, it was the petting zoo, the train ride and the pony ride, every day they did this. Sometimes they would meet Mommy in the City for lunch, Christina loved NYC and the subway and visiting Mommies work. Eddie would pick up the boys around three and they would rotate watching their sister until Karen got home from work.

Karen and Eddie had true love, they would make love and float off as one, melting with each other, as they went to that very special place. Every time they kissed, it was the same, just like the first time. There were, of course, those hectic times when she would pass him in the hall, pinch his ass and tell him to meet her in the bathroom for a quickie. They both were very sexual and he had no problem bending her over the sink for a more Neanderthal like session of sex. They met while both going through divorces from their first significant others.

Eddie's first marriage started out while he had been living in an apartment complex with his girlfriend, Cheryl. She came from an extremely dysfunctional family, like himself. She witnessed her father physically abuse her mom, unlike in his family, where his mom was the abuser. He worked as an activist for an environmental political action, which subsidized an extra room for them to house traveling activists. He also traveled the country, working on various legislation and campaigns. While In Iowa, working for Sen Tom Harkins Campaign, he was off and exploring with a friend at their Iowa City office. He had received a sonogram of his son Frank from his girlfriend. About to cross a dangerous train viaduct, across the Iowa River, he balked and said, "I can't." His friend encouraged him, "C'mon, don't be a wimp, we'll make it across, even if we hear the train, we'll have time to make it." Eddie explained to his friend, "I can't do things like this anymore, I'm going to be a father and in fact, I can't travel anymore, I want to be there for him, all the time and not miss anything".

He returned home, gave his notice and made wedding plans. Eddie wanted to do the right thing and thought it best for his son. Eddie and his first wife, Cheryl, had their differences, he felt he made a Nobel effort but working different shifts to avoid child care led his wife astray. Less than three years later, she cheated on him. She wanted to move in with her new lover and wanted to have sole custody of their son. He didn't care about any of their stuff, he just wanted to share their son equally, it was the right thing to do and Eddie always tries to do the right thing. The agreement they came to, after the judge's suggestion to his wife, was 50/50 shared custody.

She got all the stuff, he got the apartment but she insisted on a child support payment. Eddie's lawyer said no, since they both must provide equally and had been making the same salary. Eddie wanted out of the courtroom and a way from lawyers, so he said yes, as long as she bought his clothes. This would come back to haunt Eddie. They shared custodial and spoke every day, for Franks benefit.

A year or so later, as Eddie had become like the Mayor of the complex, since he had been there a while and fixed the complex up a bit by landscaping, creating vegetable gardens and flower beds. Eddie and his son Frank would share with everyone in the neighborhood their veggies. On one occasion, Eddie gathered all the kids, he called them the "Mozzarella Crew". A gang of five-year old's, he would play games with in the courtyard. Most had blond hair and he thought they just looked like mozzarellas. He was going to show them the benefits of growing your own food. It was broccoli and he explained how we can snap off a crown and pop it right in our mouths, so he did. With six enthusiastic 5-

year old's looking on, he felt and tasted something that wasn't right. They asked what was wrong and he looked at the remaining broccoli to see a half caterpillar wiggling about, the kids also saw it. They began to laugh, hardy laughter and roll around the ground, like little firecrackers popping off, like only little kids can laugh! It was worth it and he would do it again, to produce one of his favorite sounds, one of the best sounds known to man, a child's laughter. The mozzarella crew had two new recent members added, they had played whiffle ball with them and they witnessed the hysterical worm eating event but Eddie hadn't met any parent or parents.

A few days earlier, a neighbor came to speak to Eddie about the laundry room and the fact, disturbing to her, that someone was leaving their clothes in the machines for hours at a time, he explained, "I'm not an authority here and I'm sure that they must be busy multi-tasking. When I see clothes in the machine, I place them on top and continue with my own laundry." He was busy washing clothes the next day and sure enough, she was right, clothes had been left in the machine and so he placed the clothes on top and continued with his and Frank's. While drying and folding, a beautiful woman entered the room, he thought she made the machines stop but it was his heart. She wore a dress, with legs to die for but it was her eyes that captivated him, making him speechless. Beautiful, greenish blue and looking back deep into his, time stopped, they stood there in awe of each other, in love, at first sight.

He was wearing sweat pants, sweat shirt and a ridiculous NY Giants fishing hat. He stumbled through his words, "Hi, I'm um, um, an idiot and you are so beautiful, I'm sorry, new mouth, I'm just getting used to how to use it and as you can see, speak again". He smiled. She said, 'Hi, I'm Karen, thank you. I don't know about that hat but you got a great deal on that smile that came with your new mouth." That was it, he was in love. His smile widened and then she went to the clothes, he had placed on top of the machine and Eddie said, "Oh those are yours?', she cut him off, "Yea, I was out with my kids, I love to be out having fun with them laughing and enjoying living because life is short, I want them to be happy." Eddie was blown away and thought living, laughing and loving, I like that. She explained she had two boys and described them to him. He explained, "I know them, they're the new members of the "Mozzarella Crew", they saw me eat the worm." She laughed, "So, You're the local farmer who showed my kids how to eat caterpillars, they are still laughing at you, which was very nice of you." Eddie said, "What can I say, they are very welcome. My name is Eddie, some think I'm the Mayor around here but the kids think I'm a comedian, any time, it was gross, I still taste it but I do anything for a laugh, especially when its kids, they got that special kind of laughter." She put her clothes in the drier and said, "Yeah, they do." She too, was in love. Their smiles mirrored each other's, as their eyes locked then she said, slightly shaking her head, as if to clear her thoughts, "Well, I better get back to my boys, I'm a single mom, and they're alone." They returned to their apartments and he called the neighbor, who had complained about the clothes being left, "I just met the leave the laundry lady, it's the new kids in the neighborhoods mom, Mike and Derek's Mom, she's hot, I need a date, I think I just fell in love with her." She had met her earlier that day and said she would call and see what was up. She called him back and told him, "You need to go over there, knock on her door and ask her out, Courtney (HS complex resident and local babysitter), can watch all the boys." So, he did and they went out that night. They had a magnificent night. With no time to make a reservation. There was an hour wait to get in the restaurant. The moon was full, they went by the car and put the radio on and he asked her, "Would you like to dance?" She said, "I would love to ".

They danced in the parking lot to Van Morrison, under the moon light, just like the song. After, they got back ,at her door, she wasted no time waiting on him to make a move and said, "Kiss me", it was magic, he felt like play dough, she felt a warmth she never felt before. Suddenly the door opened three little boys, like parent's waiting for their daughter to come home from her first date, in unison shrieked, "Ewe, their kissing, close the door, quick." The door slammed, she pulled him in for another kiss, it seemed to last forever and they both wanted it to. They dated for a couple years, she was amazing, doing all kinds of special things, and she loved to make him and all the kids happy. Sexually, it was like nothing they had ever felt, a perfect oneness, when they made love, they would melt in each other's arms. They would look deep into each other's eyes and float away. She went out of her way to come up with elaborate gifts and romantic adventures. Once, creating a fictitious pick up for him with his car service.

On Valentine's Day, his client was to be on the tarmac waiting but it was her, she had a bottle of champagne, standing next to a helicopter, they circled Manhattan. They married a on a whim, they were living together. They woke up one day, both had the day off, he said, "I love you so much, how about getting married today?" She said, "I was wondering when you might ask. I would love to be your wife and no better time than the present. Like I always say, life is short, live, love and laugh, let's get old together doing just that."

They bought a house in the town where Eddie grew up in, a small town but only ten miles outside of NYC, in Jersey. They we're actively involved with everything for the kids. They both served on the Baseball Committee. Karen would tell Eddie, "Honey, you've put more hours fixing that field than you did at work for the past month." He said, "Yes, I did, I had to level off the first and third base lines, so the bunts rolled true. I plan on playing a lot of small ball with my teams, especially the travel teams. Besides that, the highest elected official in the county said our field is the best field in the county." A few years later they had a daughter, Christina, they all wrote in her baby book, she was his girl and Karen looked forward to finally having a child she could relate to more. It had been all boy and boy stuff and she was great a real trooper, running the LL concession stand and everything else boy. Now she had her future shopping partner and coffee clutching gossip mate. Life was good, she switched jobs into the City. Eddie became house husband.

They would take the kids to amusement parks, camping, Yankee games, Knicks, Ranger and on one occasion, the Mets. Karen's job had a lot of perks, they went to Shea Stadium for a baseball clinic for kids and Madison Square Garden was another, a sky box, for events and concerts. They tried to have fun all the time and any place they could find it, they went. He keeps dreaming of the way his life used to be and his dream turns into a nightmare.

Chapter 3

The nightmare begins

Still dreaming of the past, his dream becomes the nightmare and the reality he lives now but before that, they were happy, content and in love. Karen and Eddie began to speak about retirement, she said, "I see us on a beach, walking, holding hands, a grandchild on your shoulders and another holding my other hand." He said, "Yea, that's exactly what I see." Then the nightmare began, while making love he found a lump on her breast. "Honey, oh my God, I feel something here, a lump!" "Oh that", she explained, "it's a calcium deposit, both my Mom and sister had them, it's nothing." He was convinced it was a calcium deposit, like her sister and mom had. She made an appointment for a checkup and missed it. She made another appointment, she missed it as well, busy at work and with family. Karen had an infection that closed her eye and Eddie took her to the emergency room. While being treated for the infection, Eddie begged her to let them check out the lump but she hated being there and wanted to go. Finally, she went to the DR. and the test results made for a very bad day, she had cancer and the next tests showed it was spreading. Now, it was "Daniel Powter", in Eddie's head, playing "Bad day", "Where is the moment we needed the most. You kick up the leaves and the magic is lost. They tell your blue skies fade to grey. They tell me your passions gone away and I don't need no carrying on. You stand in the line just to hit a new low. You're faking a smile with the coffee to go. You tell me your life's been way off line. You're falling to pieces every time and I don't need no carrying on. Cause you had a bad day. You sing a sad song just to turn it around. Sometimes the system goes on the brink and the whole thing turns out wrong. You might not make it back and you know that you could be well, oh, that strong and I'm not wrong. So where is the passion when you need it the most, oh you and I. You kick up the leaves and the magic is lost. Cause you had a bad day"

Karen began Chemotherapy, once a week for three weeks and then a visit with the Dr. Their health provider declined her because she had changed jobs. After each visit Eddie had to go to the billing department for the shack down. She got ill, lost her hair but was still beautiful to him, they never stopped making love, even though she would say, "You don't want me, I'm bald and ugly." His reply was simple and sincere, "I honestly don't see that, I see the most beautiful woman I have ever seen, the same woman I met in the laundry room, I see inside you, through your beautiful eyes, I see our love for each other." He took care of her, with Christina, even when he could have had Hospice, he didn't think anyone could give her the tender loving care that he could, Christina helped him, saying to her Daddy, "Mommy will be Mommy again soon, if we take good care of her, with lots of love and help her, right Daddy?" "Of course, she will." he said. They shopped together for wigs and hats, with Christina's opinion to guide them, at four, she had no idea what was happening and neither Karen nor Eddie made any attempt to explain. They remained positive, they thought she was going to get well.

Christmas came and Karen wanted it to be perfect, making sure everybody got what they wanted. The boys were doing well, except for Mike, he was having a hard time with it and he didn't want to be around. Eddie, have personally experienced this, when his Father had cancer, he was the same age as the boys and he tried to tell him, "This could be the last Christmas you ever get to spend with your mom." He didn't believe that at all, he just wanted her to be happy and having the kids around her always made her happy.
It was April 1st, the lump disappeared and the Dr. was

thrilled, not nearly as much as Eddie. He asked the Dr. "What chance does she have to survive?" The Dr. said, "I give her a 90% chance to pull through." He was concerned about one specific blood test. It was seven days later and her liver failed. Toxic fluids filled her body, it had spread like wildfire. Eddie was in denial and mad at the Dr., "You said 90% a week ago, this is like some sick April fool's joke." He said there was a pill but she never got it. Eddie became angry with everything, even God. He refused to accept or even acknowledge losing the love of his life.

She was medicated heavily for the pain and began to enjoy the relief it brought her, Eddie felt she was enjoying too much. He thought she was giving up and begged her not surrender to the cancer. He told her, "I can't live without you" and "You can't go any place, we all need you. How will we all live, love and laugh without you? You can't leave us, you can't leave me, and you can't die!" He kept pleading with her to fight. "You are the one that makes us all happy, that takes us to Boston and Fenway Park, like when Frank wanted to go to a Yankee game but they weren't home, you say, they aren't that far away. Even to the World Series to see the Yankees win for my birthday, who will set up fake car service rides for my business, that turn into you waiting on the tarmac, with champagne and a helicopter to circle Manhattan on Valentine's Day? It's you that makes the kids happy every day and make sure they all get what they want for Christmas!! You are everything to them and to me, you are my life, you have to fight!!! Who will go shopping with Christina? Fight for her!"

The doctor had her come home but she needed constant medical attention, her body kept filling with fluids and she wasn't herself, the cancer had gotten to her brain, Eddie didn't want the kids to see her like that, he brought her back to the hospital. His denial was selfish, she was in great pain, she had to be heavily medicated to ease her pain, it was too late and she slipped into coma, after one day back at the hospital. Karen's mom sat next to her, Eddie was reading a book to Christina, when the nurse came to him and asked, "Could I speak to you, it's important?" He said, "Sure." They walked outside and down the hospital corridor. The nurse spoke, "Your wife's breathing has slowed, and soon she will stop breathing and pass. Do you want us to use life support? "He snapped back, "Life support, why is her breathing slowing?" The nurse said, "Mr Campagnola, the medication is going to stop her breathing, she is in great pain and we are trying to make her as comfortable as possible." Eddie went back to the room, he sat on the bed with Karen, at her side. Her eyes popped open, she grabbed his hand and pulled him close, "I love you, and kiss me."

She could barely speak, her mom right there, in awe of her final words and request, they kissed, and it was, as always like the first time, this was no different, she gave him one last kiss goodbye, for now.

Music, again played in his head, he could hear one of their favorite songs playing, "The Cranberries", "Kiss me". Karen's mom had taken over reading to Christina, Eddie walked away down the hall, thinking of his and Karen's time spent together and all the moments they shared, the song played in his head and he began to cry, uncontrollably, "Kiss me, out of the bearded barley. Nightly, beside the green, green grass. Swing, swing, swing the spinning step. You wear those shoes and I will wear that dress. Oh, kiss me, beneath the milky twilight. Lead me, out on the moonlit floor, lift your open hand. Strike up the band and make the fire flies dance. Silver moon's sparkling, so kiss me. Kiss me down by the broken tree house. Swing me upon its hanging tire. Bring, bring, and bring your flowered hat. We'll take the trail marked on your father's map. Oh, kiss me beneath the milky twilight. Lead me out on the moonlit floor, lift your open hand. Strike up the band and make the fireflies dance. Silver moon's sparkling, so kiss me. Kiss me beneath the milky twilight. Lead me out on the moonlit floor, lift your open hand. Strike up the band and make the fireflies dance. Silver moon's sparkling, so kiss me. So, kiss me, so kiss me, so kiss me."

Very upset, he wiped his tears returned to the nurse and protested one more time, "Why will she stop breathing?" "It's the meds." she said. He cried out, "Stop the meds!" The nurse explained her pain was too much for her without them. He felt completely helpless, he couldn't do anything to save her. He asked her mom and dad about life support and they said, "No life support, Eddie, you have to let her go." He told the nurse no and she passed away, moments later.

He had to make memorial service arrangements, Karen's mom helped with the funeral cost but wouldn't be around after. In complete denial of what happened, he had to cater this event, he hadn't begun to accept what happen, wanted nothing to do with a memorial and had nobody to help him with it. His brother's wife, Roseanne, had passed away the year before, his mom flew up to help him, and she paid for the caterer and hall for after the funeral services. He had a $500,000 life insurance policy and his mom helped him. Karen and Eddie were close to his brother's family, they spent weekends with them at their upstate NY home. They had a lake and they had some good times there. Karen and Roseanne spoke daily, Eddie and Karen were very upset to have lost her and attended every day of services for her. His mom and brother didn't show up for Karen's services. Eddie had no life insurance, in fact the medical insurance was denied for her cancer. To him, he felt, he must be garbage to them, not worthy of getting love and support at a time where it is essential. All Eddie had was his daughter that, like himself, didn't know what was happening. Somehow, they got through it, well, they had to, time just goes by and that's that, you have no choice. They just missed her very much and all they could and would do was cry together. Eddie was in denial and was unable to explain anything to his daughter.

Chapter 4

Stand by me

Six months later, all things considered, they were doing fine, except for crying a lot. When Christina was sleeping, Eddie would hold the pillow, as if it were Karen, bending into fetal position, he would cry uncontrollably. It was Eddie and his girl, with his son, Frank half the week. They did the same things they always did, their routine the same, except without the morning chaos and the after-school rotation of brothers watching her. They still did tea parties and he read her books but he also began to sing to her to put her to sleep. Two songs a night, "My Girl" and "Stand by Me". Every night. Christina would cry, "I miss Mommy "and he could only join her in tears and say, "Me too, baby, me too." They finally went to the Doctor to get a referral for a Grief Counselor, they got that and he also gave him Ativan, a drug, he said, "Like Valium or Xanax." If he should be stressed or become overwhelmed, he suggested taking those. Eddie was miss-informed, they weren't like Valium or Xanax but more like a sedative to him. He was making dinner, as he always did on Sunday for his Uncle Danny, Frank was there too and Christina was standing on her chair next to him, helping him make meatballs. Eddie's Uncle Danny called and explained he would be late and wouldn't be able to pick up some things from the store, Eddie had asked him to. Eddie had taken two pills, since his Uncle is mean and abusive to him and makes him feel bad about himself, he was intending on ignoring him. He had to go to the store and Christina had to go with him, she suffered severe separation anxiety since losing mommy. He couldn't go to the bathroom without leaving the door open, she was very afraid of losing him, like Mommy. Eddie forgot he took the pills. They shopped and got what they needed after visiting the toy aisle, it took longer than expected. Forgetting he had taken the pills.

He had made a mistake, a very big mistake to forget something like that. They got to check out and he felt like he had walked into a brick wall. The store manager had noticed him, he thought he was drunk. He went to the car feeling like he was passing out or falling asleep. He put Christina in the car and tried to drive but hit the cart he had left. He pulled back in and parked again, removed the key and told Christina we had to walk home, "Daddy doesn't feel well, I can't drive, it's ok, and we can walk home." He didn't feel well and when he got out of the car to get Christina and walk home, he noticed the police pulling in and the manager pointing to him. "I saw him driving, he's drunk and he has his kid!" The next thing he knew, his daughter's biggest fear was happening and the worst visual he could ever create was implanted in his mind forever. Christina was throwing herself at him, stuck in the policeman's arms, tears wailing out of her eyes like ocean waves behind her eyeballs! Eddie was arrested and charged with DUI. They took him to be processed and Christina to the house to see who could take care of her. His Uncle was there and he offered no help, saying, "There is nobody to take care of her, the mother is dead and the grandparents are in Florida." They had no choice but to call Child Protection Services and bring her to foster care. Eddie was brought back home, the police found out he had recently lost his wife and decided to not bring him to jail. When they got there, he met the Division of Youth and Family Services or DYFS case worker, who wanted him to sign something acknowledging that they took Christina to foster care. He took the pen, furious, still feeling the effects of the drug, he tried to stab the woman with it. The police held him back and suggested, it wasn't a good time and he could sign another time, he would never sign any document for them. There he was, home, all alone and high, He wasn't thinking clearly, he was over whelmed with the events that had just taken place and the situation that now existed as a result. Alone and feeling he had let down Karen and thinking he had lost Christina forever, like he had lost her, he took the rest of the Aadvin.

The night they took Christina, Eddie's mom, finding out what had happened from his Uncle, called the neighbor, she had a feeling something was wrong with him and asked her to check on him. Sure enough, he lay unconscious on the floor. She checked to see if he was breathing or had a pulse and found nothing. Thinking he was dead, she called 911, they came and revived him. It was three days later, he had survived the suicide attempt. Two pills got him a DUI but fifty-eight more didn't kill him, a miracle.

He was in ICU, when he came to, he was pissed off, he couldn't believe he was still alive, and neither could anyone else, including Doctors. Some thought it was a miracle, to think, he took two pills and got a DUI, how could sixty not kill him? His mom had flown up immediately and was at his side, obviously, riddled with guilt, apologizing for not being there for him. Frank, his son was there too, he was mad at his Dad, understandably, he was deeply hurt and said, "Dad, didn't you think about me and how I would feel if you were dead?" Eddie was so sorry, "Please forgive me, Frank, I was overwhelmed and I was still high from the pills I took that gave me the DUI. I love you very much, I'm sorry, I will never do it again. I'm still here and we will figure this out, together." He couldn't really explain his state of mind before he took the pills. He tried to explain, "I just know I had lost my two girls and I knew that losing me was Christina's biggest fear, I was distraught and I was all alone with the remaining pills. Now, I'm even more overwhelmed. They have Christina in foster care. I want her to get word that I am alright, I haven't died like Mommy and she is going to see me soon." He appealed to his son and my mom, saying, "It is going to be very difficult for me to get Christina back.

I need all your love and support. I've challenged DYFS in the past and they don't like me, as it is. I'm a single Dad, who had a DUI and a suicide attempt but I have to get her back." With a priest, the church lady came to visit, only family and clergy can visit ICU. Eddie had come to know the church lady through baseball, she had a son that played and was friendly with his son Frank, her name was Fran. Fran was the church lady, a somewhat extremist follower and worker with the Roman Catholic Church. Both Frank and Christina attended her vacation bible study at the church. Fran offered Eddie her help, she wanted to get Christina out of foster care and into her care. He desperately wanted that too, he agreed, it would be better, even though he felt Fran was an extremist and his daughter didn't know her that well, it would be more than any foster care. Besides that, Fran was the only one stepping up to the plate. She contacted DYFS and Eddie asked the case worker to get his daughter into her care and eventually, after clearing her, they did it. Fran immediately began to attend to the child protection certification requirements to become a foster parent and be eligible to adopt.

Eddie couldn't be released from the hospital for some time, his survival was still at stake. He had severely damaged his kidneys and he was failing tests they were giving him, he needed to pass to be released. Finally, after a month in the hospital, he was cleared, his kidneys were healing themselves. He was moved to another hospital, this was what DYFS wanted in order to be reunited with his daughter, a mental hospital. This was just the beginning of the reunification process, which would be like jumping through hoops for them. They have a time frame for reunification of fifteen months, Eddie had already wasted a month. He was evaluated by Doctors but they found nothing wrong with him because there wasn't anything wrong, he had some sad, bad things happen to him. He was overwhelmed and he had nobody to offer love and support or to help deal with any of it.

He lost his wife, his daughters Mommy, she was four-years-old and he had to explain those things to her and it was challenging. He had searched for help and was getting it but he got pills at the same time and that's what caused the incident. He forgot he took them and got a DUI.

The child protection case worker came and got him in the hospital, it had been over a month and he was going to see Christina. They met at a diner, they hugged for, what seemed like an eternity, neither of them wanted to let go and they cried, she was so happy to see him and obviously he was more than happy to see her, to hold her. He was afraid she didn't think he was alive. She didn't want to leave him, she cried hysterically, he did also but tried to assure her that it won't be long until they are both back home together. Christina was brought to Fran's and Eddie went back to jumping through hoops at the mental hospital. The intake report DYFS did on Christina, described a perfect child, after all, she was perfect, loving, engaging and smart but she missed her Mommy and now, her Daddy. Eddie felt that this was an isolated incident and that they shouldn't be a case for DYFS. That night they should have let her stay home, he never would have had another incident, he felt, and they had been through enough as it were. If they hadn't taken her, he never would have attempted suicide.

As a parent, Eddie always gave all of his time and attention to his kids, his son was a fine young man, as a result, a straight "A" student in one of the nation's premiere prep schools, his daughter was receiving the same parenting. He gave her all his time and attention to his children, he felt that was the way for them to feel good about themselves and be happy with who they were. He felt that giving them attention made them feel important to him. Everything his parents did that he learned was wrong, he made a point of not doing. He was determined, as a parent to end the cycles of abuses that had been going on in his family for countless generations. His children were happy with who they were because he made them feel important, never saying no when they wanted his attention. He did everything child protection or in NJ, DYFS wanted him to do. They drug tested him three and four times a week, he passed every test. After completing inpatient and outpatient programs, five months after the DUI, he had a court date. They tested him four times that week, the night before, he went out, and he saw friends and did a couple lines of coke. Thinking they had tested him four times that week, they couldn't possibly ask for a fifth but as the judge was ending the proceeding, the prosecutor asked for another. Eddie turned to the public defender and said, "I took a test every day this week, I'm not doing another." He answered the judge stating, "My client has taken three times the normal amount of drug tests, as my other clients, including, every day this week." The judge insisted or it would be considered a failed test, Eddie failed the test. All the work he had done for them, to get his daughter back, wasted. Does that make him a bad parent, negligent or abusive? Shouldn't he be judged on his behavior and his track record as apparent? Aren't child protection services in place to prevent or stop negligence and abuse? He has used recreational drugs his whole life, his son was sixteen and a straight "A" student, never neglected, abused or hurt in any way, nor his daughter or step children. Where they lived, Eddie served the community's Recreation Department, he was a member of the baseball committee and coached several levels of baseball teams, basketball and soccer teams, as well. He even was his son Frank's class coordinator, the new name for class mom, since he was a dad. When did the legislature vote on a law that said if a parent tests positive for, what is a taken liberty in the first place, recreational or non-pharmaceutical drugs, they can't be parents? If we tested every parent in the he USA, we would need a lot of foster care.

Eddie and Christina had some memorable visits, while she was fostered by Fran and he was allowed to visit anytime. Eddie created some great moments, he hoped she would remember. He took her to Broadway to see, "Beauty and the Beast" They had so much fun, she rode his shoulders through Times Square, pointing out the Marque to him, "There it is daddy." Pointing down the street to the theater marque, proclaiming "Beauty and the beast". They sat in the tenth row, she was afraid, having seen the Beast's picture in the lobby. The Usher, a six foot 6 African American man, noticing Christina's fear, promised her that between him and her daddy, she would be safe and that he would be sitting in the aisle, to reassure her. As soon as she saw Belle appear and break into "Good Day", she began to sing along. Then "Be our Guest", and they brought down the house and the curtain closed, she exclaimed, "It's not over Daddy?" he said, "No Baby, it's just the intermission. Now we get to go back to the lobby and buy you a souvenir." They took mass transit into the city and on the way back to Jersey, they past the Amtrak boarding area, Eddie thought about getting on a train and heading to Canada, but thought otherwise and returned to Christina to Fran's house. On the bus, she asked him to sing to her, the songs he would sing to put her to sleep, "Daddy, sing "Stand by me" and "My girl", he did and his girl feel asleep on his lap, he looked at her and he could see her mom, he began to cry.

Christina continued to view him in the same way she always had, with high regard and confidence. At Fran's house, during a visit, Fran had broken a tool and while trying to fix it, Christina suggested, "Let my Daddy see it, My Daddy can fix it, he can fix anything." Maybe because she made him sing "Stand by Me", to her every night, the lyrics stuck to her. He was able to fix things but he wasn't doing a very good job in the eyes of DYFS.

It seemed there was more to DYFS's excessive prosecution of him. None of Eddie's family members showed any interest in the case. Fran's family and especially Fran were very involved and interested. Fran had claimed god had spoken to her and was giving Christina to her.

Eddie and Karen also, had a previous situation or case with child protection, in NJ, DYFS, before Christina was born. Child protection had received an anonymous phone call with several accusations. They came to their house, unannounced and wanted to check things out. Eddie was with the three boys doing homework in the living room. He allowed them in to investigate, without a warrant. He knew the allegations were unsubstantiated. They could see, the house was spotless and the cabinets and refrigerator were filled with food. He allowed them to speak to each of the children and they were satisfied with the visit and convinced, there was no abuse or neglect of any kind. However, as they were leaving, they said his wife and he needed to go to their office for something more. Eddie was furious and I let them know it, saying, "I allowed you into my home, unannounced, with no warrant to investigate unsubstantiated claims, which are obviously outrageous and you can plainly see are untrue. I prove that the accusations are false and now you disrespect me and want to harass me and my family further. Get the fuck out of my house and off my property now!" Child protection took them to court and Eddie read the first, fourth and sixth amendment of the bill of rights, which they were violating, aloud in the courtroom. They were upset that they had to take them to court and now Eddie was telling them, they violated the bill of rights. A clerk actually asked him why he didn't cooperate and go to the office as they asked him. A simple answer for her, "I exercise my rights, like we all should and they needed to be reminded of them, nobody should think they are above the constitution." They changed the workers initially assigned to the new case, Eddie and Christina were assigned the same case workers involved with their first DYFS case, which Eddie made take him and Karen to court, and they were out for revenge. Although he had made a mistake, with the failed drug test, in DYFS's eyes, their judgement of him was not about parenting or his behavior but what he did with his adult time, away from his children or maybe it was revenge for forcing DYFS to take him to court several years earlier. Eddie still felt, who is this government to tell him what he can put into his body, as long as nobody is hurt? His DUI was an isolated incident and was from taking prescribed meds, he never had a problem before and never with recreational drugs at all. He felt, he was out with adults, what does this have to do with his parenting ability with his daughter? Why do we allow this taken liberty, without legislation, DYFS acts above the law?

As a result, he had to do an outpatient program again, he completed it. He never used any drugs again but they claimed failed tests, for other reasons, they lied and were about to railroad him in court. With nobody showing any support or stepping up in his family or even showing up for his court dates, DYFS felt it better for Christina to be in a home with several family members, who show a lot of love and support. Anne's family was showing that they could do that, her mom also lived in their home.

Eddie's son wanted to testify, he said, "Who could be better than me to tell the judge about you?" He was right and they knew it, they also knew, he would hurt their case. He was a straight A student at one of the nation's premiere Prep High Schools. They wouldn't allow it.

Fran had been working on adoption, she claimed God came to her and told her he was giving her Christina, evidently, God does not consider everyone involved or what Christina and Eddie had been through and the relationship they had. DYFS also changed their case outcome projection to adoption and they always get what they want. Fran, inexplicably and without any reason, stopped visitation and eventually all contact between Christina and Eddie.

Before the final court, Eddie voluntarily entered an inpatient program, one more act, on his part to show the courts his determination and resolve to be reunited with his daughter and he completed the program. He also went with Christina for a Psych evaluation, and when the DR was done, said she, "I will do everything I can for reunification of you and Christina. "Neither she nor her evaluation showed up at court. Nobody from Eddie's family showed up to support him either, he was all alone. His son, Frank, was also not allowed to testify, there was nobody to confirm Eddie's ability to parent. Frank, was the only person who could truly testify about his past and present ability to parent. He technically and actually failed only one drug test out of over 100 plus tests, the public defender equated it to a test in school, and he said Eddie scored a 99 plus. Enough to stop reunification?

The court ruled Eddie was unfit and Christina was soon adopted and not allowed to communicate with Eddie again. "Who is that going to be good for?" he protested. "You stole my girl from me. Where is the abuse or neglect? The DYFS intake report describes a perfect child!!" He yelled at the judge, "Why can't my son testify, where is the Psych evaluation?" the judge slammed his gavel, threatening him with contempt.

There was nothing he could do. He felt as helpless as when his wife, Karen, had passed away. Eddie's Public Defender Lawyer said because the Psychiatrist and or her evaluation never showed they would easily win an appeal, they immediately appealed the ruling but he had lost Christina. With no love and support, he cried alone.

Chapter 5

Soul-Searching

Since being hospitalized and released, followed by losing Christina, Eddie, who finally was getting the proper care and addressing his issues, continued going to grief counselling at cancer care. It was three years after losing Karen and he had integrated the loss into who he was." He started out saying, "I can't move on!" His therapist, Mark, a spiritually experienced therapist, who had previously worked with HIV patients and their relatives, explained, "You're not going to move on, what does that mean anyway? It never happened, you were never married and had a wife named Karen? You did and we will make her a part of who you are, so you will take her with you, when you go." Mark was an even-tempered person, grounded, soft spoken and very spiritual. He had searched out and experienced a variety of spiritual outlets and he shared his experiences with Eddie, they had a connection. He was interested to learn and grow spiritually under his guidance. He taught him ways to meditate and breathing exercises. He helped him arrange for his daughter to see a counselor at the same place, a therapist who worked with children but Fran, now Christina's adoptive parent, stopped taking her after a couple of visits. This was very upsetting to Eddie and others at Cancer Care, he thought he and his daughter could have some sessions together but that would never happen.

Not having Christina or being allowed to communicate with her was still a problem for Eddie and he was unable to deal with a solution, since he couldn't communicate with her. He didn't think there were problems, he believed in solutions, making this situation frustrating and painful to him, it caused him to worry and created unneeded and unnecessary stress. None the less, with his daughter, Christina, having been adopted (the appeal pending) and his son going off to college, he had nothing but time on his hands. Mark, his therapist, at grief counselling, suggested he do something he always wanted to do but never got around to. He had always wanted to drive across the country.

He figured he could start the trip with his son, Frank. Their relationship strained but repaired after the suicide attempt, they were still best buddies and he gave him more attention than ever, he needed it, he had put his son through a very rough experience. He coached his final youth baseball team, they had more fun with that team than any other team he had coached for him. Frank was about to graduate HS and he had a friend, John, from a school in New Orleans stay in New Jersey. His High School networked with other schools of the Silesian sect and Eddie became friends with John's parents. He called John's parents and explained that he wanted to go with Frank on a road trip to New Orleans, they said, "We would love to show Y'all round but Y'all gonna have to stay with us, in our house. New Orleans can be a hard place to get round and it's much better to stay with locals." Eddie agreed and he planned the logistics for Frank and he to get to New Orleans, where Frank would fly back to Jersey and he would continue on to California.

They started out by driving straight to Washington DC. They had been there together earlier that year, Eddie took him to a lobby event for" Invisible Children" a group working to help children of Uganda. He wanted to show him, first-hand, how the democratic system worked and how we, as citizens, can lobby politicians to pass legislation. They got to meet with their Senator, Frank Lautenberg. A proud moment for Eddie, he led the NJ contingency and created the three part script for the group to lobby their representative's with. He had Frank begin the presentation and as he spoke, at the long conference table, to the senator from NJ, Eddie became emotional, he couldn't contain the amount of pride he felt for his son, who was not afraid or intimidated by speaking to a man of great power.

When they were finished lobbying, with their presentation to the Sen, they asked him to take a photo. The Senators assistant spoke up, "Sir, we don't have time, they are waiting for us on the senate floor" but the senator said, "Nonsense, we always have time for young people who are here to lobby for peace." As they lined up for the photo, Senator Lautenberg put his arm around Eddie and said, "It is a wonderful thing, this democracy but it's a special dad who takes the time to teach his children, first hand, how it works. I only wish that every parent could do it, you are an exceptional dad, thank you." Eddie thanked him for his kind words but thought to himself, if only he knew, the NJ child protection people were taking his daughter away and without any neglect, abuse or abandonment. He hadn't been involved in politics since his son was born, he missed the feeling of empowerment that kind of work gave him and he was happy to see his son being empowered by it now.

Before they left Washington DC, Eddie had inquired about working for the group and he had brought the paperwork, this time, to drop off at their office. After doing that, they took pictures by a couple of Washington DC monuments they had missed during the previous trip. Eddie had begun a video diary of the road trip, posting video clips on Facebook.

They then headed to Florida to visit with Eddie's mom, Frank's Grandma. Frank had never been invited to her house, even though she had his brother's son and daughter there many times. To him, in retrospect, that was just more directions to the dumpster, even though he didn't know that's what it was at the time. Not only was he garbage, it would seem, so was his immediate family and his kids not good enough to visit his mom, unlike his brother's kids. He felt, however, he couldn't go on this trip and pass her home, while heading to New Orleans. He thought he would be a better person and go there anyway. Although his mom had, in effect, saved his life, by calling his neighbor and having her check on him, her guilt was short lived, she stayed a week in NJ, visiting Eddie in the hospital and then returned to Florida. She wouldn't help with Christina and the DYFS situation, she claimed she couldn't take care of Christina. She would help pay Eddie's rent, so they would return to the same home upon reunification, while he attended to DYFS demands, which according to DYFS, Eddie fell short of doing.

He wanted to tell Frank about his childhood during the road trip. He wanted his son to know that the families on both sides had many cycles of abuse. That he had ended the abuse that had gone on for countless generations. He wanted him to know for future reference and since they were going there and Frank never spent much time with her, he tried to explain, "Frank, I want you to know that I raised you very differently than the way I was raised. There were things my parents did that had a negative effect on who I am and I made sure that didn't happen to you. I want you to remember, for when you have your kids." Eddie knew that his son had no idea what he was talking about. He finished, "It doesn't matter, and you'll do fine. I want you to know, I love Christina and you more than anything. That's why I gave all my time and attention to you, so you would feel important and good about yourself and I didn't get that when I grew up." He was on the brink of manhood and Eddie was worried, he told him, "I had lost my dad at your age and I don't know how to be a dad to an adult. I don't know what to expect out of myself"

So, they went to visit Eddie's mom at the golf cart community she lived in with her husband Ray, who has been taught by his mom to hate Eddie and he's not shy about expressing his hatred towards him. Ray, along with Eddie's uncle, disturbed his son, who once asked his uncle, when he was ten years old, "Uncle Danny, why are you always so mean to my Dad?" He felt the same about Ray. Eddie, his mom and son went to a ball game, in Tampa Bay, The Yanks vs. devil Rays and they survived the visit with Eddie's mom. Her husband was bed reddened at the time, so it made it a little easier for them, they didn't have to go any place or spend any time with him. They got back on the road.

They were psyched to get out of there and head to New Orleans. Frank drove, as they sped off through Alabama and Mississippi. Eddie peeked over at the speedometer, Frank was doing 90, Eddie had a suggestion for Frank, "Hey, Frank, we don't want to have to spend any time here with the local Sheriff Billy Bob Wilson for speeding through his county, especially being Yankees. Some folks down here in the south still hold resentment towards northerners, since they lost the civil war." Frank slowed down to the speed limit. After spending a few days with Eddie's mom, he was in a rush to get away from her too. These states were beautiful, it was spring and they were in their most colorful bloom. Eddie wanted to take it all in, he felt he too was in bloom, he felt reborn, all new inside, his soul was searching for a new chapter and it had begun.

They arrived in New Orleans, Eddie felt as eighteen as Frank was eighteen, they were bonding like never before. Eddie thought, this is something every dad should do with their son for their eighteenth birthday, a road trip to New Orleans. They found the address and there was indeed a welcoming like no other, they had plans for them. They were immediately taken out to eat, for some real authentic Cajun style cooking, Craw dad, crab and shrimp, with their heads and lots of it!! Eddie went bar hopping with Frank's friend's dad, Dan, while Frank caught up with his friend, John. Dan had to work the next day and pinned his address on Eddie's chest, he wasn't much of a drinker, he was feeling drunk and a cab took him home later, and he got sick. Between the food, excitement and booze, Eddie rarely drank and shell fish had, in the past, gotten him ill, his stomach couldn't handle it.

He recovered well and woke up the next day to a "Pig Roast". Their New Orleans friends had a huge party planned and they had all the trimmings and a Southern Rock band too!! Frank was having fun with his friend and Eddie was enjoying everything else. They had a blast but it was time for Frank to fly back to Jersey and for Eddie to continue to head west.

Eddie took Frank to the airport, he saw him off and then he drove to Houston, to visit with his brother, Roger and his wife, Mary, whom he married less than a year after his wife Roseanne passed away, evidently, he was cheating on Roseanne with her.
The visit with his brother was great, he showed him around the city of Houston. They went to an Astros game together and also drove to Galveston, for a day trip. On the way, Eddie was disgusted, when driving by Texas City, nothing but oil refineries, the sky was an ugly yellowish urine color, he could only describe it as the asshole of the country.

While Roger worked, Eddie was able to ride his brother's bike around and explore on his own. His wife, Mary was regimented and he felt, she was mean to his niece, Autumn. As she did homework with her, actually calling her stupid. He was disturbed that his brother allowed this. When it was time for him to go, Mary said, "Eddie, you are the best house guest I've ever had, respectful and clean, I hardly noticed you were here. You are welcome here any time". Eddie always tries to leave things a little better than the way he found them. He was grateful and appreciative to them for a pleasant stay. Houston is not a place he would want to live but it was nice to spend time with his brother, whom he always felt was his friend and not just his brother. Before he left, Roger asked him if he planned on going to San Francisco, he said, "I hadn't planned on it but the idea is a good one and I will consider it." Roger had a parting gift for his brother, a copy of jack Kerouac's "On the Road".

As he headed west, the landscape changed dramatically, across the state of Texas, from Bayou Country, a low lying, very wet region with elevated road ways, to dry plains and then mountains on the horizon. He stopped in San Antonio, to visit the Alamo and the river walk that is a man-made river with shops and restaurants, nice but Eddie felt, it was, what it was, fake, manmade, very fake.

He wanted to get to San Diego but stopped in Las Crucias, NM and then again in Phoenix AZ. Along the way, the site seeing was amazing, the mountains and desert, too much to take in by passing by just once. The serenity of driving alone and taking it all in without saying a word was therapy no therapist could provide him. Breathtaking mountain ranges, north-west by south-east, extending over these lofty plateaus and balls of hey rolling around, like the lost souls of the earth, just rolling in the wind and dust across the desert. These mountains look like broken spurs, some, to Eddie and his sexual one track mind, he thought resembled giant vaginas carved into the continuous ranges. There are narrow valleys, wide open plains between the mountains, deep canyons and gorges, in every direction. Then, rock and desert, cactus, until deep into California. The sky was even more amazing and the effects the sun had on the landscape, changing the colors of the mountains as it crossed over the sky, surely, Eddie felt he would find his reason for being, his souls' purpose amidst all this beauty God has manufactured. He traveled route 8, through Yuma, mountains to his right, Mexico to his left. Past Mexicali, he's in a valley but he begins to climb, he wonders if the minivan can handle this trip. Up these mountains, he has a hard time keeping his eyes on the road and his ears are popping, as his hearing goes in and out, with the ups and downs, these mountains are truly majestic, like the song says.

Then back down, he senses his last decent from the mountains to ocean into Chula Vista, where he will stay, just outside San Diego, where he plans on wetting his feet and then heading back east.

All the while, talking to his friend, "Billy from the Bronx", who's in SF and his tempting offer to stay by him, if he decides to drive up the coast? Eddie's brother, was also determined to convince him to see San Francisco and the North Bay, where he assured him, that he would fall in love with the region. He agreed to drive up the coast and would take two days to do so.

He stopped in Hollywood and spent time walking the sunset strip and having a burger at the Roosevelt Hotel, he just had to. Then off again, driving and trying not to drive off a cliff, the minivan shaking and telling him to be careful. The waves crashing into the rocks below, less people on the beach as he surged northward to his artsy city destination. He stopped again in San Louis Obispo. He's been reading "On the Road", by Jack Kerouac, he's got a copy of it on the passenger seat next to him. His brother gave it to him in Houston, it's inspired him since San Antonio to be a free spirit and roam the country. He finds a local paper that is celebrating Kerouac and the time he spent there. He spends the night there, in honor of him and reads a few chapters, he feels he can deeply relate to the main character, Sal Paradise, who, in the book, starts out on his journey where Eddie grew up and spent his life, Paterson, NJ. The story has motivated him and he is feeling a spiritual connection to the author, Kerouac. Feeling an excitement like never before, he felt free, his soul search was giving him a feeling of being spiritually reborn.

It's the next day and he's back on the road. Monterey, just up ahead, it's time for lunch and then only a few hours to San Francisco. He made it, the minivan makes it, what a ride, he's blown away already and he just got to the "City by the Bay", where he's about to fall in love with it.

His friend, "Billy from the Bronx", worked in "The Haight" and it was easy to get directions to the most famous part of San Francisco. His friend, that he has known since he moved to Jersey from the Bronx in grade school, had been trying to convince him to visit. Eddie couldn't wait to show his gratitude and thoughtfulness, he was very happy he took his advice and drove up the coast, an amazing logistical adventure, filled with the most breathtaking scenery in the world. He was working at a bar called "Zam Zam" a bit of a dive in the Haight, just a block off Ashbury. He showed Eddie around the city and across the Golden Gate to the North Bay and the Redwoods, it was everything he was told it would be and more, just like the drive up the coast. When he worked Eddie crossed the bridge again, fascinated with the region, where the bay ended to the north in Petaluma and the small hippie towns, like Sebastopol and Cotati. This was the place for him and he wanted to live there. It was time to go and he expressed his feelings to his old friend, Billy from the Bronx", "This is where I want to live, I'll be back." In his head the music played, "Going to California" and he understood completely the lyric, "How could tomorrow ever follow today?" He had to go back east but his spirit had been revived, he was a completely new man.

He was heading east now, back home to New Jersey, he had some stops planned along the way. First he stopped in Las Vegas. It was night time and he went to the "Rivera", where the "Rat Pack" hung out. He went to the bar and ordered, "Bartender, Tequila, please?" and at the same time, in the section of bar next to him, he heard the same request, at the same exact time. He looked over and it was a woman, a smoking hot, age appropriate woman, with blond hair, a beautiful, well-kept body and a gorgeous smile. They toasted with their tequila and as Eddie was looking at her, a man slipped in next to him and between the woman and Eddie. The man said hello and explained that he was in town for a bachelor party. Evidently, his friend was an idiot and was breaking up their crew by getting married. Eddie asked him, "Does he love her?" He gave him a blank stare and Eddie realized, he was himself when he was twenty something and had no idea what love was. Eddie explained that he had been married twice, the first time was because his girlfriend got pregnant and they tried to do the right thing but it didn't work, probably because they weren't in love. Eddie then went on to explain how he met his second wife and began to elaborate how he felt about her and also that she had sadly passed away. The man was as uninterested as Eddie would have been when he was his age, Eddie was understanding and recognized this.

The man said good-bye to Eddie but before he could do the same, the tequila woman was on his stool. Saying to Eddie, "I couldn't help eves drop on your conversation with that young man." Eddie said, "That's ok, he's young, he didn't understand what I was talking about. I wouldn't have either, when I was his age." She introduced herself to him, "I'm Dina, from Petaluma California." Eddie became visibly excited, "Petaluma, wow, I just left there, I visited a friend in San Francisco and just fell in love with the region, I told my friend I'm going to move there, I'm Eddie and I live in New Jersey but not for long." She was beautiful, he thought of "Going to California" again, omg, she has, "love in her eyes and flowers in her hair", he thought, is this happening again, love, could I possibly have found love again? She was excited to talk about his wife and interrupted his thinking, "It was so beautiful they way you spoke about your wife to that man." Eddie replied, "It's easy for me to do that, I loved her very much, it was very hard for me to lose her but I've been through therapy and I learned how to integrate the lose into who I am, she's a part of me now and always will be with me." Dina was blown away by his sincerity, "I hope to find love someday and hope someone will speak like that of me." They were looking deep into each other's eyes as she said that and Eddie was getting that same sweaty palms and strange feeling in his stomach he had when he met Karen in the laundry room, he said, "Well, no better time to start that than the present. Do you know how beautiful you are? I want to know more about you and Petaluma, come to dinner with me?" She said, "I'm in Vegas shooting pool in a tournament, I'm sorry, I'm tired and need sleep." He suggested, "How about tomorrow night?" They said good night and they exchanged numbers. He thought about her all night and into the next day and then she called, they met and went out for dinner, it was amazing, they had a fantastic connection, they picked up right where they left off. The two were feeding each other, conversing and laughing as they talked, they were so comfortable with each other's company, and everything seemed so natural. After dinner they went to see the light show on Freemont Street, the original Vegas strip. They were on a terrace having cocktails, he was thinking, how or what do I have to do to kiss her, what should I say? She was probably thinking, why doesn't he kiss me? At that very moment, a woman approached them, she had cameras hanging around her neck and she said, "Hi, excuse me but you two look like you are so in love and I'm creating a photo essay of couples, would you mind kissing while I take your picture?" Eddie couldn't believe what she asked, is this an insane coincidence or what? He asked Dina, "Would that be ok?" she said yes. The kiss was amazing, fireworks were going off in both of their heads, and they melted and just kept kissing. They left, walking hand in hand, she asked what he wanted to do now and Eddie said, "To be perfectly honest with you, I want to make love to you all night long." She was a little bit taken back but she felt the same way and said, "That's a great idea." and they proceeded to her hotel and did just that. When they got to the room, she said, "There's a bottle of tequila and limes on the table, pour us each a shot. I want to change." She grabbed a few things and went into the bathroom. Eddie cut the lime and poured the shots. She came out all in white, sexy stockings, with garter and corset, lace bra, she was fifty but had the body of a twenty-year-old. They toasted their tequila, once again, kneeling on the bed, Eddie took her glass and placed it on the end table, then slowly their lips met again and again they began to melt in each other's arms. He laid her down and his leg slid up in between hers, as they kissed again, their lips fit perfectly together. They made love all night long. They went to that place, he thought he would never go to again. In the morning he told her "I have to be honest, I've been asking myself, if it's better to have loved and lost than to never have loved at all but I never thought I'd be asking myself if I was in love again." I have only been with a couple of women since my wife's passing. It's been three years, for the first two years, I watched our home made porn and masturbated, I made the mistake of sharing that with a friend and my friend insisted we go out and, as he said, pick up chicks. I met a woman and we had a one night stand. I felt like I had a separation of body and spirit. It was like my spirit told my physical self to go ahead and do what you got to do,

I don't want any part of this. Having truly loved, my body and soul knowing what love is, makes anything else seem pointless."

They spent the next four days together. He watched her shoot pool and they made off the charts love as much as they could.

Eddie was in love again, Dina was sharing the feeling and for her first time. They both departed Vegas, she went west and he east and he couldn't help feeling, he was going in the wrong direction. He passed the Hoover Damn and every sign that said east was telling me, it's the wrong way.

He visited a friend in Albuquerque, New Mexico, an old friend, Dick. Dick was his best friend in High School. They had spent a lot of time together back then, cutting class, chasing girls and playing music. Dick had beaten cancer in his twenties and moved from NJ to the cleaner air and environment out west. He played the drums and they reminisced about the old days in NJ. Eddie shared his Las Vegas experience with him and Dick suggested he take it slow, knowing how Eddie would get head over heels for girls back in HS. Dick reminded Eddie about what Mark, his therapist at grief counselling, had told him. He wanted Eddie to contact him if he ever met someone he was romantically interested in, Mark had said Eddie could be vulnerable to deceit or a scam. Mark thought Eddie might think he had found another like Karen and have expectations of the same relationship he had with her but Eddie ignored the suggestion and never contacted Mark. The two old friends went to a concert together and Eddie departed for his next stop, Memphis Tennessee.

In Memphis, he went to Graceland, Elvis had nothing on Eddie on this day, as he was in a special place in his mind and in his soul. He went to Sun Studio, Roy Orbison was no longer singing to him, he had said good bye to being sad and lonely, his spirit was soaring and

his life blood was tempered with love. Dina and he spoke constantly and he described the sites he was seeing and how he felt he was going in the wrong direction, he wished she was with him. On to Nashville, more sites, "The Grand old Opry", he was amazed at all the Cowboy boot and hat shops, Downtown Nashville offered, where he grew up, nobody wore either.
Back on the road and getting closer to his home, New Jersey, he drives across the Blue Ridge rolling hills of Virginia and his last stop, before NJ, in Williamsburg, VA, to visit yet another old friend. They went to the historic reenactments, having fun and joining in with the actors who were playing the parts of the American founding fathers. His spiritual searching journey was coming to an end but he thought he had found what he was looking for.

Finally, he was back in New Jersey but knew it was just a matter of time before he went back to California, this time to live. It was June and his son's graduation from High School, he has been accepted into Marist and he had prepared him for college. He was more than confident his son would do well. His mom was not so nice to him, and after graduation, told him she didn't want to speak to him anymore and that there was no reason to. Eddie didn't agree but thought, whatever, he was enjoying seeing his sons' success and had moving to CA on his mind and said, "I'm sure there will come a time that we will need to talk. If you need anything at all, ask me. I will keep paying child support, for him at school."

Dina and he spoke every day, as he began to plan his move to CA. He rented a place in Novato and had already lined up work with the basketball referee's Association, as well as with the soccer association. Summer was over, his son off to college and he loaded up the van with everything he could fit in it. He was going to California, as usual, the music played in his head... "With an aching in my heart, somebody told me there's a girl out there with love in her eyes and flowers in her hair." He had already met her, life was good, and no it was better than that.

He spoke to his son about the move, his son didn't want to prevent him from the experience and he was going away to college anyway. Eddie told him, "I have to follow my heart, I always have, I hope you have the courage to follow yours as you experience life and gain wisdom. I will pay for you to come visit soon. I love you more than anything, I will always be there for you, and I'm only a phone call away. I'm so proud of you and everything you have accomplished. You are a man now, go be the all the man I raised you to be." Eddie cried, he knew they were very close, best Buddies, they had some bad things happen, out of their control but they made it through.

He didn't want to say good bye to him, especially with him moving 3,000 miles away but he had to follow his heart. Eddie had one problem, that he couldn't address, his daughter. He doesn't normally refer to anything as a problem, only solutions and with love a solution can always be found. In this case, he couldn't access the solution because all lines of communication were shut off by Fran. There was nothing he could do, for the time being, it would have to wait.

Chapter 6

Going to California and Californication

It was 11 pm eastern time and Eddie was leaving for CA, the next day, in the morning. Dina and he were on the phone and she said, "I have something to tell you." In Eddie's experience, this is not usually followed by a good thing. She continued, "I'm married." This would be the first of many red flags she would wave, in fact, she had more red flags than the UN has flags. He was following his heart and was convinced by circumstances and his feelings that they were meant to be and in love. Even though if Dina was married, in Vegas, she was planning on being with someone, after all, she had to have that "Victoria Secret" hottest white, fuck me now lingerie with her for a reason. He also didn't consider that he might be vulnerable.

He set out the next morning as planned, he searched for his soul, he found it reborn and free and now he wanted to find the ultimate. This time, he drove straight out there, on route 80 and he reached the Mississippi at midnight. He was in Iowa, where Dina grew up, she moved to AZ at 16 and when she was 17, moved to CA. She had her first child, Fly, while in HS.

Eddie made it to CA in four days. Eddie met Dina and they stayed in a hotel, picking up where they left off in Vegas, melting into one as they made love all afternoon and into the evening, when she had to leave. She explained that her husband and her had been separated but living in the same house. They slept in different rooms and were in the same house for logistical purposes and for their kids, who were now in their twenties, two daughters. Then came more red flags, she said, "I have a boyfriend, we've been together for six years but she had already told him, that she didn't want to be with him anymore. Still, Eddie was undeterred and felt their love for each other could overcome any obstacle but the obstacles kept mounting. He started to work right away, refereeing Varsity, HS soccer. He was accepted well by the two associations in the region and had two games a day, in Sonoma and Marin counties, a JV game and a Varsity game. He had also become a rec basketball official in the town he had moved into and he officiated games at night. In California, there is an enormous about of people involved in playing sports and Eddie was able to make a living just by officiating. Dina began to introduce him to her friends, the first a "fuck buddy", the second, the same and the third, yet another, only this one would pose as her husband and they would go swinging together. Red flag after red flag, the UN got nothing on her when it comes to flags. Eddie joked, saying to Dina, "Why don't you tell me if you haven't fucked somebody when I meet them, since I haven't met anyone that you haven't fucked yet."

He apologized, even though she chuckled and he said, "You are the woman I fell in love with, you are who you are and I love unconditionally." With that, she said, "I don't like living this way, it's extremely stressful, between the deceit and scheduling all this sexual activity, not to mention the cost of hotels for the rendezvous. More importantly, I found you and I've fallen in love with you and I want to change the way I've been living." In two months, she told her husband, had broken up with her boyfriend and ended all other relationships. She wanted to live completely honest. Dina and her husband had owned a property, adjacent to the bus depot and future site of a new train station. The train was to commute passengers from SF into the North Bay but the time frame kept changing and they were unable to keep the property. They had to sell it but as part of the deal, Dina would stay on as Property Manager. The property had a couple of barns on it, one was used seasonally for Halloween and fireworks but

the other she collected rent from a man who was a collector of sorts and he sold clothes and other items there. Dina introduced Eddie to the man and this time, for the first time, she didn't mention that they were sexual partners. His name was Harald Sigurdsson, he had a full beard and mustache and looked exactly like the famous Viking his name sake might have looked like. Eddie and he had an instant connection, they could talk for hours. Harald was amazing in Eddie's opinion and his vast collection of things fascinated him. They became good friends, Eddie asked Dina to be sure to include him, whenever she had to visit him. He didn't know if they had been sex partners and he didn't care or think about it. Harald was special to him and Harald held Eddie in the same regard.
Eddie and Dina moved in together into a one room cabin, with a loft. There was a fireplace, our only source of heat and they would sit in front of it often. He loved to see her glow, in the light of the fire, he adored her and worshiped her. They cooked together and danced around the house, their song, "loving cup", by "The rolling Stones" and they felt that beautiful buzz, together. They had a run off that flowed under their cabin, Eddie would pan for gold, being from NJ, he thought the gold was everywhere in the region. He would think he found some and bring it to her.

Excited about a potential find, he would say, "Look, Baby, I found gold!" Trying to let him down easy, she would say, "Well, that's not gold but there's a lot of fool's gold. The gold was actually found a couple hours' drive from here but keep trying and maybe you will get lucky." He said, "I found you, I couldn't be luckier." He kept at it and after he found more of, "his gold", he would place it on the window sill. When he got to showing her, "his gold" for the twentieth time, she said, "Yes, Baby, that's gold, colored, put it with the rest of your gold collection." They would laugh, as the sill became filled with his gold. They were one of five houses on the property, which was like paradise and they were like Adam and Eve. There were beautiful flowers and lilies in the creek. An abundance of fruit trees, that produced fruits from June to December and they had a vegetable garden, they maintained together. A deck was outside their back door, up the stairs from there, a hot tub and the next level, an antique bath tub and a sauna/steam room. He would draw baths for her, with lots of bubble bath and give her a sensual bath. He would slowly, gently glide the luffa all over her body and then join her in the tub. They made love constantly, they began to take the feeling of oneness and joy with them, after they made love, and it would last for hours. He would go with her to shoot pool in the league she played in and she would come to his games. He was training at camps and became friends with, Rafael Santana, the region's best and most well-known trainer for Officials in the North Bay. When attending his summer camp, Dina baked treats for him to take for everyone at camp.

They would go places together and with friends, the blissful couple were in a world of their own. At the beach, they wouldn't ever pass up on the possibility of an intimate moment. They made love, with the ocean cracking its waves on the rocks beside them. In the vineyard on a blanket with the moon and stars shinning above them and they always took notice of the beautiful surroundings all around them, here in Sonoma County, CA. They were both having the time of their lives, they had found the ultimate.

The paradise they had found, the joy they felt, were real and their love was powerful but temptation, like Adam and Eves was about to be presented to them. They had found the ultimate and the power of having it went to their heads, they were about to use it for the wrong reasons.

Eddie received an e-mail from the Uganda lobby, they wanted him to come to Washington DC, to train with the group that would be working in the field, in Africa. He declined, having found the blissful paradise he was experiencing, he had to, he thought he had found the ultimate and perhaps he and Dina had done just that. It had been one year and the best year of each of their lives, after all they could tell you how Adam and eve lived.

Then bad news, Eddie had been in touch with the lawyer who was handling the appeal for his daughter's child protection and adoption case. He wasn't allowed to attend the session but was confident and so was the lawyer, that he would win an appeal. Without an explanation, he got a call, it was over and he had lost, that's all she could say.

His tears were uncontrollable, his hurt immeasurable, there was nothing more he could do and he searched for an escape. He asked Dina about finding recreational drugs, He needed to self-medicate. Unknown to him, Dina had been using since he met her, Meth Amphetamine. Also, unknown to him, was that it was Harald Sigurdsson who supplied her with the drug, they went to visit him, they got some and Eddie snorted the crystal, after crushing it. Not only did it help him to not feel the emotions of the moment, it made him, extremely horny and uninhibited, something he didn't need to enhance.

He was now more intrigued by Dina's former sex life, especially swinging and he would ask her to tell me some stories of her exploits. He didn't know exactly how it happened but before he knew it, they were swingers. Dina may have manipulated their new activities but he was a more than willing participant. They were both ready and willing to do anything sexually they could think of or be introduced to. Crazy and wild couples would join them, other men, for three-some's and sex clubs in San Francisco. They were out of control and their drug use got worse. They would get hotel rooms in SF and party with anonymous, women, men and even Transsexuals. They had become try-sexual, meaning, they were ready and willing to try anything, at least once and they did just that. They had some rules, they didn't kiss anyone, they stayed together in the same room and they didn't communicate with anyone, after the encounter. This was their apple, the temptation that ruined paradise for Adam and Eve was about to do the same to them. They gave in to the devil, who rules this world now and whose job it is to destroy love. As always, music played in Eddie's head, "Black Sabbath" "Lord of this World". "You're searching for your mind, don't know where to start. Can't find the key to fit the lock on your heart. You think you know but you are never quite sure. Your soul is ill but you will not find a cure. Your world was made for you by someone above but you choose evil ways instead of love. You made me master of the world where you exist. The soul I took from you was not even missed, yeah. Lord of this world, evil possessor. Lord of this world, he's your confessor now. You think you're innocent, you've nothing to fear. You don't know me, you say but isn't it clear. You turn to me in all your worldly greed and pride but will you turn to me when it's your turn to die?"

It wasn't long until, Dina went and met somebody from one of their encounters, by herself. What they were doing required a higher level of trust and breaking that trust was that much worse, Eddie was devastated. He had invited his son, Frank and his girlfriend and they had to pretend that everything was ok. At first it was but when Dina didn't want to go to the city with them, for a Giants game, they had bought tickets for, they had a fight in front of them and it was ugly. Dina wanted to stay home, get high and who knows what else. Their whole relationship got ugly. She had begun to smoke the Meth and he smashed her pipes.

They continued to stay together but they were doomed. Months later, while having dinner at Rafael's, he asked if they knew anybody that would be interested in renting his extra room. They didn't know of anybody but said they would ask around. In the back of his head, Eddie was thinking about saying he needs to rent it but he didn't want Rafael to know about their difficulties. Eddie waited but things didn't get any better between Dina and he, she began to disappear and wouldn't say where she was or who she was with. Clearly, she was no longer being faithful to him. He feared she had returned to her promiscuous ways again. Paradise, it seemed was lost for them and by themselves and their own greed, temptation and pride had destroyed their once blissful love for each other. They had everything, they had the ultimate and lost it. Eddie's relationship with Dina had gone very bad, like Adam and Eve, they were paying the price for biting the apple, Eddie thought they were finished and had to move out. He felt he gave all of his love to her and she wanted something else or maybe she just enjoyed the rush she got being deceitful. Like the shoplifter that has plenty of money but shoplifts anyway, to satisfy some other feeling. It was two years since Eddie came to California, he thought his soul search for the ultimate had been more than successful and it was, their last kiss, was the same as the first, they still loved each other but they had experiences that hurt each of them deeply and they didn't think they could recover from them.

Chapter 7

A Golden Opportunity

Eddie's friend, Rafael, who was a full time Sports Official, umpiring D1 baseball, refereeing D2 basketball and HS volleyball, he had all seasons covered, plus he was paid to train by the HS associations and ran training camps. He had a son, Ian, whom Eddie shared a birthday with, he was exactly 40 years older than him, and they had an amazing connection, even though he was just a little kid.

Eddie called Rafael and he asked if he had found anyone to rent the room, he hadn't and said he would be happy to rent it to him. He moved in immediately. They enjoyed each other's company thoroughly and Eddie worked for his Association, North Bay Perfect Officials. Eddie had been officiating since 2001, with the exception of soccer, mostly Sub Varsity and Recreation level but since being in California, he had become a Varsity Official in Basketball, Baseball/Softball in addition to Soccer. He had stopped using drugs and was feeling all the emotions he had been hiding away, being around Ian, brought back memories of his son and thoughts of his daughter, he thought of them every day and he missed them very much.

He would speak to his son, who was doing well in college, now a junior at Marist. They spoke on the phone often and he would send him pictures of his daughter and updates on how she was doing, he was doing a decent job of keeping his and his sisters dad, Eddie, aware of how she was and he knew it meant a lot to him, it was all he had.

After a couple of months, Rafael, seeing that Eddie worked hard and had to hustle to keep a steady and extensive Sports Official schedule, asked him if he wanted to Officiate at the college level? Naturally, he did. Rafael told Eddie, "You will need to do two sports at the college level to be able to live comfortably." It was obvious that soccer would be one, as Eddie had played in college and was most comfortable refereeing soccer. He knew the game well, felt at home on the field and had his most experience, both Officiating and playing it. He also had already been assigned Varsity Soccer play-offs. The other sport, to advance to the college level, would be baseball, his favorite and the sport he played the most growing up. He had only played basketball up until the eighth grade. They began training, physically and theoretically. Rafael would have him stand in front of a mirror practicing his "mechanics", the term they would use for displaying signals. Rafael would move his arm or turn it to the position it should be in to accurately convey the call. He said to Eddie, "When it comes to verbally communicating, you need to drop the NY minute, be clear concise when relaying the information to the scorers." Eddie would talk fast and sometimes confuse the scorers. They videotaped and would watch, Rafael would give Eddie constructive criticism. One time pointing out how cool he was, "Look at you here, wandering around by the scorer's table, like "Joe Cool", I'm wondering, at what point you are going to put your two thumbs up and say AAYYYYEE, like "Fonzie", from "Happy Days" that old TV show." He was fun and poked good fun at Eddie. "I love this one, hands on your hips, I'm Super Ref." He trained him on the coffee table positioning Officials and players using Ian's toy figures. He was easily able to translate basketball into soccer, they are relatively the same, just a bigger scale. They would go to the gym and run or bike outside, he would do the same sit ups, pushups and chin ups, as Eddie, except once he had him run up and down this hill a dozen times, Eddie said, "Your turn." Rafael laughed and said, "I'm not running up and down that hill." He was getting the training people would pay a lot of money for and Rafael was doing it for free.

He was a great man, magnanimous, one of the best men Eddie would ever come to know in his life. Eddie didn't have the ability, stability or balanced equilibrium he had but he saw aspects of him that had great potential, smart, fast and an ability to know what was going on, whether on the court or field. Some Officials can make calls, see fouls well and know whose ball it is but don't have a clue what's actually going on in the game that hurts their ability to preventive Officiate. That means to see things before they happen and do or say something to players to prevent it from happening, that was Eddie's strength and it made him a good Official, Rafael recognized that.

Eddie was being evaluated for HS basketball playoffs, he had to score below a 2.0, and the scale went from 0 to 4. Early on in the game the foul count was 3-0 and Eddie told his partner that the fouls were uneven. Sometimes a team just fouls more but in this case the team with no fouls had some advantage fouls that were let go. He called a fourth foul, Eddie let him know now its 4-0, and then a fifth and Eddie said, "5-0 on fouls, look for something on black." Inexplicably, his partner called a sixth foul on white, Eddie didn't even think it was a foul. The white coach erupted, Eddie switched position with his partner, he was now by the scorer's table and the coach came out of the box. Eddie ignored him. Rafael said to them at half time, "Did either of you know what the foul count was?" and Eddie's partner volunteered saying, "Yes, Eddie told me when it was 3-0, 4-0 and 5-0. Rafael said, "Why did you keep calling fouls on white?" He said, "I thought they were fouls." Rafael replied, "Fair enough". Then he asked Eddie, "Eddie, why didn't you do anything when the coach was outside the coach's box yelling at your partner?" He couldn't lie, "I'm sorry, I thought the coach was right." That gave him a 2.1 in his evaluation score. On the way home, with Eddie, Rafael said, "All you had to do was say, Coach, I need you to get back in the box." Lots of

Officials make calls and don't understand what's going on and that a coach is about to explode. Eddie learned his lesson, these lessons were hard, and he didn't get playoffs that year in basketball. However, everything was going well, with soccer officiating. He had been assigned play-offs and advanced to the Junior College level in soccer, until one night.

Eddie was sleeping and he was awakened by rocks hitting his window, he looked down and it was Dina. They had spoken a few times but she had returned to the lifestyle she was leading when he met her. Seeing her there sent a chill throughout his body, he was still in love with her. He ran down and let her in, Rafael had no problem with her and didn't know exactly why they split up and Eddie didn't want to disclose his part involving the breakup, either.
They kissed and it was just like the first kiss, when they met in Vegas, she came up to his room and they made love, melting and going off to that special place again, they both missed it very much, that beautiful buzz. They began seeing each other again.

Across from the property they lived together at, where Dina still lived was a vineyard and they would walk, talk and always take a blanket to make love a mist the grapes. The way the warmth of the sun felt and its setting in the horizon across the field of grape vines created a soothing and mellow atmosphere perfect for a romantic walk and the ultimate setting for love making. It was different for them now, she wasn't about to be loyal to him and was honest in her self-appraisal, when it came to sex, she wanted to be as promiscuous as she was when they met.

The training with Rafael continued, it was 24/7. They would spend one night a week on the court together, so Rafael could train Eddie as it happened. It was at the Bay Club in Marin and the players were high level players, most had played in college and were still in their twenties. Eddie's strained relationship with Dina continued, as well and it was affecting his ability to focus, Rafael knew what was going on, as Eddie had been sharing with him the short comings in his and Dina's relationship. He told him about her promiscuous lifestyle and inability to be monogamous. It was at the Bay Club, during a game, when Rafael became upset, saying, "I need you here, Eddie, on the court, where are you?' What could he say other than the truth, "It's Dina". He never told Eddie how to live his life, he said, "Eddie, you know she's not just shaking it for you." Eddie said, "I know, I know." But he couldn't stay away from her. One weekend, while Rafael was away doing a four-game baseball set at the University of Hawaii, Dina spent the whole weekend with Eddie at Rafael's house, they were partying heavily, a friend and fellow Official stopped by, it was obvious what they were doing and it got back to Rafael. He approached Eddie about it. "People would pay a lot of money for the training, mentoring and advancement you are getting for free because of me. I don't tell you how to live your life or who to fuck but she's no good and she's fucking you up. On the court she's filled your head, if you can't focus and decide what you want, her or a career, I'm telling you, if it's her then we are done." Eddie told Rafael, "Go fuck yourself." Rafael swung at him, they were fighting, and Eddie got Rafael in a head lock and was punching his head. He stopped, he couldn't believe what was happening, he told him, "I'm letting you go, I don't want to fight with you." He let him go and Rafael swung hard, putting Eddie's nose on his cheek, saying," If you get high in my house, I could lose my kid, get in the car, I'll take you to the hospital." He was right, Eddie deserved it.

He fucked up, again and he said, "I don't know why I sabotage things like this? I'm a good person, loving, caring and helpful. How did this happen?" Eddie felt it was time for him to leave California. It was just like the song, playing again in his head, "Going to California", "Got a punch on the nose and it started to flow, I think I might be sinking. Throw me a line, if I reach it in time, I'll meet you up there, where the path runs straight." The next day, he met Dina, they made love one more time, amazing as usual. Later on, Harald met them and Eddie got some speed for the trip. Eddie said, I have to go, I'm not sure what I'm doing or exactly where I will end up but I got to go." He hugged his good friend and he kissed Dina, as always, it was just like the first kiss and he drove off the next day, with just enough money to get to NJ.

Chapter 8

Back to Jersey

It was February and the rains were still falling, with "Sweet Virginia" playing in his head and eerily, just like the lyrics go, he was living it. "Wadin' through the waste stormy winter and there's not a friend to help you through. Tryin' to stop the waves behind your eyeballs, drop your reds, drop your greens and blues. Thank you for your wine, California, thank you for your sweet and bitter fruits. Yes, I got the desert in my toenail and I hid the speed inside my shoe." It was exactly like that for Eddie. He spoke to his mom and was going to visit her in FL on his way to either his friend Drew in Virginia or back to New Jersey. He went to Vegas, it was Valentine's Day and he ended up with a woman, they had sex but Eddie wasn't into it, he did the speed and it happened but he ran out of speed and somewhere in Arizona, he got sick. Eddie ended up being held up in a motel 6 for four days. It was a nightmare, fever and puking, he was in hell, physically, in addition to his already emotionally distraught state of mind. His mom had left Florida by the time he was back on the road, now he desperately needed to see her, as he spent most of his money, needed for his travel expenses to get to NJ, on Motel 6. His mom was going to Biloxi; MS and he was to meet her there. He got there at noon, on fumes, the tank was empty. He was a mess. He had four hours until he had to meet her. In the van he had a cooler, with a six pack, he went on the beach and drank, then passed out. He woke and he had to find a bathroom fast, there were people on the beach. It was a long walk and he didn't exactly make it. He went up to the casino, where he was to meet mom, she wasn't there yet. He was filthy, had sand and piss all over him and he smelled. The only clothes he had were a suit, still in plastic wrap from the cleaners. He asked the bell boy if there was a place he could freshen up and he directed Eddie to a locker room, with a shower. He shaved, showered and put on the suit. It seemed he would be able to pull it off, somehow, he did it and he actually looked good, great, all things considered. He was ready to meet mom and there she was." Eddie, what's going on, you look good but are you ok?" "Yea, Mom, I'm fine." If she only saw him about an hour ago, thank god she didn't. He said, "Let's play some cards." She gave him a hundred dollars and they went to the three-card poker. They were losing, he had twenty left and so did she. She slid her twenty to him and said, "I'm going to try some slots." Next hand, he got a straight flush, eight hundred dollars. He gave his mom the hundred back and had his travel money, to get to NJ. He spent the night in her sweet and head east the next day. On the way, his friend Drew said it wasn't a good time, so it was off to Jersey he went. He spoke to another friend, they offered him a live-in free property maintenance gig. He accepted and was home again, in New Jersey. He fixed up the place real nice, mostly landscaping and he was umpiring baseball and softball all spring and summer, his new skills and ability blew away his old officiating colleagues. That fall, he officiated soccer and was given two rounds of playoffs, he was clean and sober. Fran still wouldn't let him see his daughter, Christina. He did get to see Frank, he went up to Marist to visit it him, they hadn't seen each other since Frank visited him in CA and was witness to the end of his relationship with Dina. They were happy to be in each other's company again and it was good to have a catch again, Eddie missed him and he missed his dad. Frank came to Eddie's place also, Eddie made a mini golf course at the property, and they played and had fun. He was still in love with Dina and thought of her daily, he knew it was just a matter of time until he called her, to at least see what she was doing with her life. Then, Dina called and they began to speak regularly.

Eddie loved and missed her and she still loved him. Winter came, Eddie hadn't seen snow in a few years and it was his job, as part of the maintenance of the property, to shovel the property. In February, Dina said, "I'm coming to NY, I arrive at JFK Valentine's day." Eddie picked her up, it was seventeen degrees, and she didn't mind and was just happy to be with him and him with her. The kiss was still like the first one and making love still took them to that place, they had bliss again. Even though we messed things up in CA, Eddie thought, clean and sober, it would be different in Jersey and it was for a little while. Eddie didn't know it but she had brought meth with her and when she ran out, she got sick, like he had in Arizona.

Eddie didn't know any where to get Meth in Jersey, it's not a popular recreational drug in NJ and the people he knew didn't do it. He did know where to get coke and so he did. He thought, just to get her through coming down from meth but that wasn't the case and they both started doing it a lot. That led to the same lifestyle drugs led to in California. Now it was "Bad" playing in his head. "If you twist and turn away, if you tear yourself in two again. If I could, yes, I would if I could, I would, let it go, surrender, dislocate. If I could throw this lifeless lifeline to the wind, leave this heart of clay, see you walk, walk away, into the night and through the rain, into the half-light and through the flame. If I could through myself, set your spirit free, I'd lead your heart away, see you break, break away, into the light and to the day. To let it go and so to fade away, to let it go and so, fade away. This desperation, dislocation, separation, condemnation, revelation in temptation, isolation, desolation, let it go."

You would think they would have learned from the first time but obviously, they didn't and they bit the apple again. The same results followed. They were both doing well in NJ, Dina had gotten a great job working in NYC and Eddie had a part time job delivering school lunch, while advancing rapidly with sports officiating.

They were using cocaine and attending sex parties and once again, arguments concerning respect for each other, drugs and their individual behavior returned, over whelming them. Something that can be expected at the sexually explicit engagements that they attended. Dina treated Eddie like he was her bitch. They had planned to go back to California together, both of them had jobs lined up. She was in Jersey through the summer and left Eddie in September.

He stayed, he stopped using again and he was assigned a HS final for soccer. It was exciting and professionally, he was back on his feet. Losing Dina, hurt him and he wasn't well in his heart he was heartbroken, after the split up, he wanted her back. He thought it was the drugs and if they were clean and sober it would be different. Since she had come to NJ, they had gotten an apartment and they were both working. She had a great job working in NYC, on the upper west side, with the dual income it was do-able but after she left and he couldn't do it himself. Eddie's mom helped him pay the rent for one month, well, she was giving him money his dad had left him, that she was supposed to give to him but never did.

Either way, she asked him to come to FL, they needed to work out their differences. So, he gave up the NJ apartment and headed for FL. It had been many years that he and his mom were butting heads and it needed to end. They had a lot of issues to discus and he was excited about straightening things out with her. They each held a great deal of resentment for many years. Eddie needed her now, like never before, he was lost. He had found himself and his soul but somehow found himself right back where he was after losing his wife, Karen and then Christina. It had been an emotional roller coaster ride, for Eddie, since his wife, Karen had passed away, he was looking for some calm stability. He had soul searched and became reborn, he had found the ultimate and lost it. Even then, he was given a golden opportunity and he blew it. He and Dina tried again, their love was still alive but once again, they gave in to temptation. Eddie was searching again but he didn't know what for. He thought his mom could help him with some directions to Happy Street, nothing complicated, perhaps something simple, he didn't want the ultimate anymore, he would be content with a place in FL, where he could officiate all year, like in CA.

Chapter 9

The Final Directions to the Dumpster

Eddie was going to Florida, to work out his differences with my mom and maybe settle down there to live. He had lived in FL before and he liked it there. The differences between he and his mom started when Eddie was very young, he was beaten by both his parents. His dad would hit him with his open hands but his mom would use weapons. On more than one occasion, Eddie had to hide the wounds provided by the belt strap, his mom would use on him. Given her position as a Program Director for the county, it would have made the six o'clock news had anyone noticed he was being beaten by her. Eddie's mom had gone back to school when he was 4 and had him start his education early. By the time he was twelve, she had completed her education, with a master's degree and had a great job as a county administrator in special education, and she was a program director. Eddie's parents would fight constantly, holidays and vacations, which for most people, were a joyous occasion, were not fun in their house. Eddie had an older brother, Roger, they would hang out together, as friends, throughout their childhood and shared many of the same friends. As adults, the two brothers continued to be friends and would get together regularly. Roger had a college degree and worked for an insurance company, he had a big heart, was caring and liberal. Until, after years of working for insurance, he became hardened, less understandable and more conservative. Eddie also had a younger sister, Emily. Emily was a special needs person, she was born blind and she was autistic. She would sometimes be picked on in school and Eddie's father would call on Eddie to "Go have a talk with these boy's that picked on your sister." Eddie would have to confront his sister's assailants and make sure they left her alone, usually by beating them up.

Eddie and his sister had always been close, he was her protector.

Since his mom had been in school, his dad had to provide for them, as well as pay his mom's way through school. Now, she didn't need him anymore and wanted to leave him. She gathered Eddie, his brother and sister for a family meeting. Before their mom could start the meeting, Eddie, now twelve years old, began immediately protesting, "How can we have a family meeting without dad?" His mom began, "Because, it's about your dad. I want to leave your dad but I will only leave if all of you come with me. We will have to move far away, since he is connected to people in "Little Italy", in the city and I'm afraid they will find us." Eddie, disturbed by the meetings premise, interjected, "Of course he will, we are his children too, how selfish of you. This meeting is not about my dad, it's not about our family either, and it's about you. You are conspiring to betray my father and you expect me to join this conspiracy?" Eddie was outraged and said, "Are you so out of touch and so caught up in your work that you think I want to move far away from my friends, with you and without my father?" He couldn't believe what was happening, she was out of touch. His dad cooked their meals, it was him whom Eddie would go to for any advice, money or anything. His mom never had any time for him, she was always busy, never gave him any attention and now expected him to take her side in a potential divorce. Eddie gave his own proposal, "How about this, mom, you go and I'll stay with dad. We'll be fine without you, it's not like you're here anyway." His Mom was extremely upset with his response, saying, "I will never be on your side for the rest of your life." Eddie thought, how could she put a decision of such great magnitude on me, in the first place? He really didn't believe that she meant what she said but she did and would never do anything for him again and would never be on his side again. Eddie couldn't wait to see his dad and inform him of this conspiracy. He got home and Eddie went out to the car to meet him, in the front of their house and said, "I have something to tell you." But his dad said, "I've got something more important.

I was just at the Doctor and I have been diagnosed with cancer, I'm going to die soon." Eddie was speechless, this was truly already a day he would soon want to forget. He turned back towards the house, as he began to cry, this was far too much for a thirteen year old, living in a violent dysfunctional family, as it was. His dad caught up with him and put his arm around my shoulder and said, "I'm sorry, I will try and fight this cancer and if we are lucky, I will beat it and stay around. I want to be there for your kids, to be their Grandpa someday. What is it you wanted to tell me?" What could Eddie say, nothing mattered if his dad died, "Nothing dad, it wasn't important. I know you can beat the cancer, you're tough and I need you, mom doesn't like me anymore." He said, "I will try my best. What do you mean your mom doesn't like you anymore?" Eddie realized he may have said too much and recanted, "I mean she never has any time for me." Eddie never told his dad about his mom's conspiracy to betray him. He was tough and he fought the cancer for several years. He was smart too, he saved all the materials list he had from his job. He worked with Asbestos and had been diagnosed with Asbestosis. Before he passed away, he gathered the family all together, for a real family meeting, with everyone present, including Eddie's mom. He explained that, with his life insurance policy, pension and other monies, their mom would be well off. His mom also had an excellent job with the county.

Eddie's dad told the family, "I have a settlement coming, from a law suit, as a result of the cancer and its cause. I was at my lawyer's office today and I'm very happy to let you know, I will be leaving you all some money, after I die. The settlement money will be split three ways."

His mom agreed with his dad. Eddie's dad died when he was eighteen. He said his last good bye and I love you to him and nobody else, in front of Eddie's mom. He had been in a coma and was expected to die at any moment. Eddie was his favorite, as he sat next to his comatose dad, on his hospital bed, when his eye's opened and he grabbed Eddie's hand, he pulled him close and said, " Eddie, you are my A#1, I love you more than you will ever know." With that he closed his eyes and passed away. His mom looked on, in disbelief of what she had just seen, envious of his dads love for him, even though it was something she had rejected. Eddie kept his mom's conspiracy to betray him a secret but he had just lost his biggest ally and advocate and he was irreplaceable. This was something he wanted to address with his mom. As well as, when Eddie turned nineteen, his mom threw him out of the house, for no reason, other than he had stopped going to college and was working an overnight union job. He had dropped all his classes, to make sure the tuition would be refunded, as soon as his mom received the check, she kicked him out. A friend and coworker of his dad got him the job, where his dad had also worked. He wasn't a bad kid, he smoked pot and experimented with other recreational drugs but he wasn't a criminal and he never hurt anyone or was in trouble with the law. Eddie was a happy go lucky, loving and caring person, always willing to help anyone in need.

At a family wedding, a cousin was getting married, there was an open bar, before the actual reception. Eddie's mom suggested he drink as much as he could, since after the cocktail hour, the cost of drinks would be out of pocket for him. He got drunk and got sick during the reception. His uncle and godfather, who had paid for his cousins wedding, was extremely upset with him and he held it against him for his entire life. Eddie wanted to discuss that with his mom, as well. After all, it was she that encouraged him to drink more but she shared none of the blame. In fact nobody even knew that she had suggested he drink more, at twenty one, he was an inexperienced drinker and one would think, his own mom would be someone who would advise him of the danger involved in drinking too much and not encourage him to drink more. He wanted to know why she hadn't explained herself to the family.

Over the years that followed, Eddie's mom did pay for certain things but with whose money? She paid to keep his home, while he attended to DYFS demands, after losing Christina and paid $7,000 for a car when he was in Jersey with Dina. He never received cash from her, she paid for things and always took the credit for doing so. The money she paid for things had to come from the settlement she got after his dad passed, he never got his third and whatever she paid, wasn't close to the amount he should have received. Despite that, Eddie's mom took credit for any monetary help she gave him even though she was really using money that should have already been Eddie's after his dad died. Eddie wanted to address the settlement money, he never received.

Then there was the flood, when his family was evacuated. His mom still lived in the house he grew up in, across town from where he lived at the time of the flood and, on a hill, unaffected by the water. Eddie had three young kids that were displaced from his home, they were scared. He told them, as he was excited about it, "Don't worry, my mom will help us." Eddie went to the house to find that his mom had left for Pennsylvania to avoid any inconveniences the flood caused her. She left them, her son and her grandson, without a place to go. She left the community, at a time when communities are supposed to come together and help each other. The next week, she called, she was upset that Eddie's wife, Karen had told someone, who had asked her why she and her family had to go to a hotel, when his mom lived above the flood line that she had left town. Eddie didn't know why his mom was upset, his wife, Karen had simply answered the question concerning his moms where bouts during the flood and she answered truthfully. Two months later, Eddie, Karen, the kids, Mike, Frank and Derek were at his mom's house for Christmas, she gave Eddie a bag of sox. This had become an annual joke for Eddie's mom but he didn't find it funny, he felt it was abusive. They all had to go to another room to see his brother Roger's' gift, a beautiful bicycle. With that, Karen told the kids, "Gather your things, kids, we were leaving". She proceeded to tell Eddie's mom off, calling her abusive, among other things, they never spent another Christmas with his mom again.

Another issue was when Eddie's brother's wife had passed away, his mom flew up from Florida, where she had retired to. For Roger, she paid for the caterer and hall for after the services. His brother had a $500,000 life insurance policy, he didn't need any help. When Eddie's wife, Karen passed away within a year after his brothers' wife, his mom didn't even show up, he had no life insurance policy and certainly needed help.

Following his wife's death, Eddie had the situation with his daughter and once again, his mom was unable to help or give any love and support, this effected the way child protection handled the case he had regarding his daughter. Family involvement is a factor that weighs heavily in child protection cases.

Surely, Eddie and his Mom had to work out some things, important, life altering events, that the effects of, had distanced them from each other, in addition to her abusive behavior towards him and the money, his father tried to leave him that he had never received. Eddie thought it was the perfect time for them to finally do this.

His break up with Dina had him broken hearted, he had literally left his heart in San Francisco.
From the second he arrived, in FL, her husband was being verbally abusive and demeaning towards him. Finding any reason or without reason to verbally attack him. He and his mom began to talk about things and were making head way but her husband kept interjecting with his needs, all which he could have done himself. On the fourth day, he physically tried to attack Eddie, without provocation, his mom had to put herself between them.

Eddie was considering living nearby and had been looking for a place, he had also found work and before the week ended, he was working. That night, her husband tried to attack him again, Eddie's mom asked her husband why he was doing that. His answer, "I just don't like him." The next day, Eddie confronted his mom, "Mom, one of us has to go, if I stay here and allow him to continue to abuse me, and I have no self-respect. If he gets past you and reaches me, I'm going to hurt him and I don't want to do that." She said that it was he, meaning her son, Eddie that would have to go, as she couldn't put her husband out. He had always had a no tolerance of that kind of behavior with Karen or a girlfriend and Karen had the same policy with him or anyone she dated before they were together. Eddie was shocked and this hurt more than anything his mother had done to him in the past. His disbelief had him in a daze, did his mom just let someone attack him and not only, not do anything about it but her solution was to have him leave? All this, while they were supposed to be working out their differences. To him, this was another life altering moment. These were his final directions to the dumpster. He didn't know where to go, except, back to California and find Dina. He was now, also, officially homeless. He had come to FL, in peace, filled with love, yearning to repair his relationship with his mom, he was searching for a calm environment, after riding an emotional roller coaster, and instead he got more chaos and was confronted with evil. He would suffer the grief from the hurt and pain that evil handed him. He was looking to simplify and live close to mom and maybe help her in the near future, as she was getting older. Now, he had very different thoughts about his mom, he had always believed in her and that she wanted the best for him but now, he was confused. As the music played in his head, John Lennon's, "Mother". "Mother you had me but I never had you. I wanted you but you didn't want me. So, I just got to tell you, goodbye, goodbye. Father you left me but I never left you. I needed you but you didn't need me. So, I just got to tell you, goodbye, goodbye. Children don't do what I have done. I couldn't walk and I tried to run. So, I just got to tell you, goodbye, goodbye. Mama don't go, daddy come home. Mama don't go, daddy come home, repeat."

Chapter 10

Homeless

Eddie was distraught, he raced to California, to find Dina. His mind was racing in thoughts faster than his car. He couldn't believe his mom made him leave, was it ok for her husband to be so abusive, even trying to physically attack and hurt him? Eddie was raised to think that mother is always right and to always believe in her. He drove straight through, the bible belt, across route ten, like he had a few years earlier, when he was in a much better place, spiritually, on his soul searching journey, sightseeing, only he didn't see a thing this time, only road. His racing thoughts centered on his mother and the bad moments and experiences over the years between them. He thought of the meeting when she wanted him to join her conspiracy to betray his father. He thought about how she was never on his side throughout any of the times he needed her. Mostly he thought about how despite all that, he had still believed in her but how that now changed for good. He recanted in his head other times where she wasn't on his side or there for him and there were a substantial amount of those times. He began to realize that she had meant what she said at that awful family meeting, without his dad. All these years he believed in her, now every event, moment and experience involving her with him had new light shed on it and things became easier for him to figure out. In essence, he had just lost his mother, she was dead to him but what he didn't realize is that she had already been dead to him and for a longer time than his dad was.

Eddie had spoken to Dina a few times but didn't know what to expect, their split up in Jersey was as ugly as ugly could be. It had been six months since their epic departure. Their last fight became physical, as she hit him several times. Eddie thought, it was the drugs and if they were both sober, maybe they could work it out and find bliss again. They spoke, when Eddie arrived in Santa Rosa, he had a motel room, she came to see him. She didn't want to kiss him, she resisted everything that was loving. They had sex and for the first time, they didn't go to that special place, there was no oneness. Dina's heart was cold and without love. After, she told him, "I've been seeing someone seriously and I'm falling in love with him.' Eddie couldn't resist the obviously non believer reply, "You have a funny way of showing it, and you just cheated on him with me. You are back to the person you were before you met me and probably worse, having thought you found love and it turning out the way it did." He continued," It was the drugs, Baby, give us a chance without them?" She wanted no part of Eddie and his pleas to rekindle their love, she received a call from a completely different lover while they spoke. It was over for good between Dina and Eddie. Eddie felt suicidal again but remembered he had promised his son he would never do that again. He was supposed to go to Marist with his mom for his college graduation but Fran told her Christina could go, if Eddie wasn't there. Eddie was forced to miss it, as Fran imposed her will, preventing a moment for Eddie and both his children to have together. It had been a long time that darkness had kept them apart and it would remain black as night for Eddie. He hated himself and he was sure his son wasn't too happy but he didn't know that Fran had imposed her will on them and his mom had rejected him.

Now, Eddie was about to renege on the promise, he didn't care about anything anymore. His mom's rejection, followed by Dina's. The prospect of seeing his daughter again was dim and he couldn't attend his son's college graduation. Too many times he has felt this kind of hopeless despair, he felt he had enough and he was not wanting to live anymore. He wanted to shoot himself but getting a gun in California wasn't easy. Nevada, he thought, on the other hand, has the most lenient gun laws in the country. He drove to Las Vegas, he made several last ditch, collect calls to his mom, and she refused them all.

He figured he would kill himself, after a big farewell party in Vegas. First, he shopped for the gun and found one, all he had to do was save $500. He went and sold the car, his mom had bought, and he wanted nothing to do with it anyway, after what had happened between them. He hired Hookers, partied and gambled down to the $500 he needed for the gun. He went back to the gun shop and when he tried to purchase it, he gave his ID and the salesman said, "Ok, we will mail it to this address." Eddie shook his head, "No, why can't I take it now?" The salesman said, "If you live in Nevada, you can walk out with it but you live in CA and it has to be mailed." Eddie thought about it, "Well, I would like to try it first anyway, in your shooting range." He was thinking he would turn the gun on himself at the range but he wasn't the first to think that, the salesman was hip to him and said, "We use blanks in our shooting range, this is Las Vegas, you're not the first to try that one." Eddie went and lost the $500 gambling. Now he had to do something, he tried my mom again, he told her his situation and his desire to commit suicide. He gave her his location and asked her to order him food, she didn't but she called police and he was brought to a mental hospital for an evaluation. He was clean and sober when he was taken to the hospital and he wanted family members to know this. He asked his cousin to view his hospital records of tests and such. He signed the release of information to be given to his cousin. Everyone had been saying Eddie's problem was drug use but Eddie knew now that that wasn't the case. He wanted to share the evaluations and tests he was given with his family, so they would be able to learn for themselves what Eddie's problem really was and it was his mother. His cousin declined and, in fact, never spoke to Eddie again. The hospital released him a few days later and he wanted to go straight to a bridge to jump off. He was now homeless in Las Vegas, a bad place to be homeless, in Vegas, they kick you when you are down. After a couple weeks and having nobody to turn to, he went to a freeway bridge and was about to jump into traffic, when, while on the bridge, about to jump, a friend, a fellow Soccer Referee, Santo called him. He said, "Come back to California, stay with me, we can figure this out." Eddie had connected with another friend on Facebook and he paid for a flight back to SF, Santo picked him up at the airport. He stayed on his couch, he got back into Officiating, he had kept the CA association aware of his progress while in NJ and they knew he had been assigned a HS Varsity final, the last season. Eddie was technically homeless but was staying at his friends, on the couch.

It was at this point when he spoke to his brother or actually he listened to him, as he called him names and ridiculed him for what happened in Vegas. Eddie didn't understand why his brother was mad at him. After all Eddie was the one who was homeless, had no car and he was the one suffering. Eddie's brother, Roger, told him to move on and stop complaining about being abused but he hadn't experienced what Eddie had. He had his uncle kiss his ass, take him places and give him things. All Eddie got from him was abuse. The same from their mother, he felt, how dare he tell him to get over it, without having any idea what it was like to be directed to the dumpster, by the same people that always showed him love and support? Eddie hadn't done anything wrong to him and it was their mom who rejected him, none the less, he and his brother haven't spoken. His brother would ignore him from now on and won't answer his calls. Eddie never got to tell his brother his side of what happened in FL, with their mother. He wondered but had no way to find out what

his mother had told his brother had happened when he visited her, to repair their strained relationship.
He continued to try and dig his way out of the enormous hole he was in. He got a part time job, working in the morning, waiting tables for breakfast. This fit in perfectly with his full officiating schedule and he was beginning to see the light at the end of the tunnel.

After his son graduated, in May and he had turned 22, he had to end the child support payment he had been giving to his son's mom. She wouldn't speak to him, for no reason. Eddie had to go through his son, Frank, to proceed with the process of ending the child support payment. He and his son, gathered the proper paperwork and each filled it out and sent it to the proper authorities, to end the monthly payment.

Eddie had set up a couple of bank accounts. In one account he put a dollar a day into for his daughter, he thought of her daily and figured he could show her that with the account and also give it to her, when they were reunited.

That October, four months later, Eddie received a letter from child Support in NJ, so did his employer and his bank. They claimed he was in the arears but it was a mistake, the payments were to be stopped that previous May. He couldn't get in touch with anyone in the child support office. He called his son, whom he shouldn't have had to do this with but his mom refused to speak to him. In 22 years, he had never said a bad word about his son's mom. He was upset about the mistake and the fact that he had to go through his son to fix it, it was his ex-wives responsibility. He had some choice words for his son about his mom, she had spoken badly about him for years but his first-time to bad mouth her, resulted in his son not wanting to speak with him again. He didn't do anything wrong, it was her responsibility and now his son wouldn't speak to him. Eddie's boss called him into the office and said, "I just got a letter from probation, I thought you said you hadn't ever been convicted of a crime?" Eddie replied, "I haven't and I got the same letter, its child support, they are under the department of probation in NJ." His boss said, "Oh, so, you haven't paid your child support?" Eddie couldn't believe what was happening, he was a class mom, for crying out loud, he was involved with everything that had to do with his son. He put more hours into fixing the baseball field than at his regular job for several weeks. Now he was being labeled a "Dead Beat Dad", by NJ. They put liens on his bank accounts, destroying them, including the one he had started for Christina. Now, he had to try to explain, "NO", he said, "I never missed a payment, they made a mistake." She didn't believe him, two weeks later, he was "let go" for some bull shit situation concerning hours that had to be cut back. Eddie finally pushed the button on the phone when child support prompted for lawyers, he got through immediately and they fixed the mistake but the damage to his reputation and his bank accounts was done.

While driving with Santo, in route to a HS soccer match they were officiating together, Eddie vented, "Ok, Bad things happen to good people but how many times and speaking of timing, I was just beginning to see the light at the end of the tunnel and everything was taken away." Santo replied, "I have some bad news too, my son may have to move back home and you are going to have to find a place." Eddie was feeling stressed out and said, "We have to officiate, we can talk later, and it's time for us to be a relaxed crew." They had a competitive match that night, the officiating crew was brilliant, Eddie was happy, he was very conscious of the calls he makes, he thought he got all of them right tonight at Center Ref and Santo agreed, "Yea, Center, you got a couple good ones tonight." Eddie laughed and said, "Yea sometimes we get them all."

His friends began to distance themselves from him because nobody knows you when you're down and out. His mom wasn't speaking to him either, he began to think about her and how she wasn't ever on his side. He thought, she's never been on my side and how he never got the third of that settlement he was supposed to get. Any money he got from her was, actually, from his dad, through her. All she ever really did was put Band-Aids on his issues, never saying here, start a business, like he wanted to. She was controlling him and abusing him, the whole time. Could she be following through with what she said when she wanted to leave his dad and he didn't join her conspiracy to betray him? Was this some sick vendetta held against me since he was twelve? Eddie and she never got to discuss these matters, since he was forced to leave. Could his mom have manipulated her husband to attack him, so she could make him leave and not have to be held accountable or provide him with validation for her part in creating his situation?

One thing was going well for Eddie, Soccer Officiating. Eddie had received two evaluations, from the assignor and the Association President, both were excellent. In one evaluation, out of six categories, he had four very goods checked off, with two goods and very little, if anything, to work on. He had been assigned college games as well. He did have some concerns and he felt he had the credibility and experience to be able to address them with the hierarchy of the soccer officials, to association. The issues, were about the other Officials and their inability to preventive Officiate. Three games, where he wasn't the center referee but the AR or linesman, with limited input, had Student Athletes removed by ambulance with broken bones. Another game was assigned to a recent graduate of one of the competing schools, in a rival game, with playoff implications. Eddie thought he unfairly officiated the game. He addressed these concerns with the Assignor and the Association President, he told them, and "I think we have some problems, I'm concerned about the safety of the Student Athletes we officiate. We need to train more and specifically, in the area of preventive Officiating. I've been AR in three games this season alone, where student Athletes were taken to the hospital with broken bones. All of those injuries could have been prevented by the center referee. Also, the assigning has been questionable, I was assigned AR to a game where the center referee was a recent graduate of one of the competing schools." Their response, was to not give him any more games, including playoffs. He was kicked out of the Association because he had legitimate concerns and brought them to the attention of the leaders of the association. The next soccer season, Eddie went to the other counties in the region to officiate. At first, he was given games, in Marin, he was even assigned a division two, women's game at Dominican University. A week later, a committee member from his former association, conducted a training class that Eddie attended. That week, he wasn't given a schedule in Marin, the Assignor wouldn't return Eddie's phone calls and emails, they had black listed him.

In one months', time, he had lost two jobs, bank accounts, his brother, his son and his mom, whom wasn't really there for him anyway. He didn't do anything wrong for any of this to happen. He found out his mom was doing her job to turn other friends and family against him, so as to not look bad after rejecting him and sending him off homeless in FL, by telling everyone he was a drug addict, he hadn't been using any drugs but that was about to change. He had no love and support at all and he turned, once again, to Meth amphetamine to suppress his feelings.

Eddie's stay at his friends was over, Santo had to make room for his son, who was having a tough time keeping up with rent, after moving into his own place. He was grateful to Santo, who helped him, for nothing in return. Santo wanted to have him stay but he had to put his family first, Eddie understood. Unfortunately, he was out on the street, alone, afraid, without a job and with no love and support from anyone.

This is the moment where the hardest slap of reality that has ever hit Eddie in his life, smacks him. This is when he realized, for the first time, when he was ready to go home, he was homeless. It was late and he was tired and it was the moment where he would head home. Only this time, he thought, "I'm done, time to go home but holy shit, I don't have any place to go. Now what?" He stayed up all night, walking around, and thinking of what to do. Eventually, he set up a camp on environmentally protected land, where he would be taken out of by police.

Eddie still went about it by loving one another. He felt the pressure associated with being on the street and "Under Pressure now played in his head. "Pressure pushing down on me, pressing down on you no man asks for. Under pressure, that burns a building down, splits a family in two, and puts people on streets. It's the terror of knowing, what this world is about, watching some good friends, screaming let me out. Pray tomorrow, gets me higher. Pressure on people, people on streets. Chippin' around, kick my brains around the floor. These are the days it never rains but it pours. People on streets, people on streets. It's the terror of knowing what this world is about, watching some good friends screaming, "Let me out". Pray tomorrow, gets me higher. Turned away from it all like a blind man, sat on a fence but it don't work, keep coming up with love but it's so slashed and torn. Why, why, why? Insanity laughs under pressure, we're cracking. Why can't we give ourselves one more chance? Why can't we give love that one more chance? Why can't we give love, give love, give love, give love, give love, give love, give love, give love? Cuz love's such an old-fashioned word and love dares you to care for the people on the edge of the night and love dares you to change our way of caring about ourselves."

Eddie was still working for Rafael, and he was worried about him, now living on the streets full time. He offered to let him stay at his place, to put together some money, instead of spending what he made on motel rooms. He had saved a thousand, lost patience and went to the local casino, where he lost it all. He couldn't face Rafael and tell him, so he left him a note and 86ed myself back out to the streets. Despite this, Rafael continued to give him work.

Eddie stayed in the light, loving one another. Anything he had, he would give to anyone. He shared everything with those on the streets, food, money, drugs or clothing. If you needed a shirt, he gave the one he was wearing. Life was hard, he camped or stayed up all night, riding his bicycle or he would go to Harald's and hang out.

On the Avenue, for a couple years, until the new casino took their patrons, Eddie hung around a place called "The Internet Café", it was basically a store front gambling casino that also provided internet service. He became good friends with the manager, Cheryl, they would hang out together, and also help out each other, with things like loaning money. She had a big heart, as well as street smarts and would advise or sometimes warn him about being involved in certain activities. Their friendship would outlast "The Internet Café" and it's run on Santa Rosa Avenue.

While there, on Craigslist, he got a job sign waving, which led to an additional job setting up an outside display on holiday weekends. Eddie wore a gorilla costume, he got from Harald. People began to associate the gorilla with the store. A mattress is a necessity item, unlike pizza or burgers, people don't drive by a sign waver and decide to buy a mattress, like they might do for a burger. Eddie felt the gorilla would be something that stuck in their heads, so when the time came for a new mattress, people would know where to go because there was the mattress store that had the gorilla. He would give balloons and take pictures, with passer byers, as the gorilla.

Since Eddie's first days here in Sonoma, there was Harald Sigurdsson, he had met Harald through Dina, and at the barn she rented to him, where Dina was the Property Manager. He no longer rented the barn from Dina.They had become good friends, Eddie was invited to Herald's place, with Dina, after she revealed to him that she did meth, she also revealed that it was Herald that sold it to her. Harald was no longer friendly with Dina but he and Eddie remained friends. Eddie continued to spend time there at the compound in Santa Rosa, with several barns, where Herald would store his collectables and peddle meth. This was sanctuary for Eddie, he began to depend on going to Harald's for peace of mind. He and Harald would sometimes hit golf balls into the pasture fields next door and there were many other things that got his attention there. Harald was usually willing to explain his collectibles. The story behind collectables is really what they were all about to Harald, who was a great story teller. He also would loan Eddie money, help him replace his stolen bicycles, give him food or blankets and help him with self-medicating. He would have a social network here also, getting to meet and know people from the nightly gathering of characters, who were like the guests on late night talk shows. The Harald Sigurdsson, chemically unbalanced late show, with topics, of a unique variety, ranging from sports, politics, one of Harald's collectibles or gossip. Eddie would get on his soap box, saying, "We have given up our liberty! I don't think anyone knows what liberty is. It's as if a waiter brings you your meal and says, here's your meal, I've taken the liberty of removing what I felt was bad for you and he puts an empty plate in front of you. That's having your liberty taken, think about that when you celebrate the fourth of July." Or sports, Harald's baseball team, the Milwaukee Brewers, herald was from Wisconsin and was a fan of "The Brew Crew", he and Eddie shared a love for baseball and its history, they would reference past players and managers often. Eddie would philosophize, saying, "I think in this life, we have a choice to be protected by either an umbrella of love or hate. Those that are under the umbrella of hate, exhibit characteristics that are, selfish, controlling, manipulative, hurtful and uncaring. The umbrella of love protects with the characteristics that are qualities, like being caring, considerate and helpful. It seems that we have to choose and there is a balance that exists and there will always be both. I choose the umbrella of love." Harald would reply, "And the Brewers are going to win the world series, when we are all under Eddie's umbrella of love" His place, this compound became and was a sanctuary to Eddie, the only other place he could go to was the local casino, which had forced the closing of the internet café, as they were unable to compete.

Eddie loved the fact that after he and Dina split, Harald remained his friend and not Dina's, it doesn't usually work that way. Most people he knew here were through her. Harald has a big heart, generous and caring. He helped Eddie through rough times and helped him to survive on the street. He reminded Eddie of a gentle version of a Warrior Viking, not the violent person his name sake was, even though he may have looked just like him. When it came to drugs, meth or anything else society has labeled bad the two felt it's because of propaganda from big pharma, they just want a monopoly on drugs. They would laugh about the pharma ads and how more than half the ad is about side effects, Eddie would mimic the announcer, "And, in some cases, may cause death but don't smoke the evil weed you can grow yourself." Eddie and Harald shared a strong belief in one thing, liberty, people should be allowed to decide for themselves. Their conversations would be considered subversive to some but to them, anybody should be able to freely do anything they wanted, as long as, nobody was hurt, including using any recreational drugs.

Eddie tried to start a small business, sign waving or what he called, "Live Performance Advertising" The Company, "Sign Slingers" offered costumed Performers. They could create an advertisement for a service, product or an event. Eddie posted five advertisements for his company on Craigslist, every day. In addition to the gorilla costume herald gave Eddie, that he was wearing at the mattress store, Harald had several other costumes in his collection of everything and anything. Harald had let Eddie roam around his compound to find a variety of things for his company. He gathered materials to make a sign to advertise for his company. He explained, "If I can sell this Advertising Company with the same method I'm going to sell somebody's service, product or event, it will prove it works." Harald couldn't say no to Eddie, his enthusiasm and ability to keep trying kept him from denying him any supplies he might need for his new venture. Harald admired Eddie's ability to keep trying, he knew how hard it was for people on the street, an insight that is rare.

Eddie ran advertisements on Craigslist for two years and he got very few clients. He got a call from the local animal rescue, they were looking for a costumed dog to promote their annual picnic, in exchange for Eddie's Company name to be given out to their mailing list, "Sign Slinger" logo on their website and his sign with logo hung at the event. In other words, Eddie was a volunteer, for a good cause. He arrived at the shelter at nine am. He dressed in dog costume and they drove him to a busy intersection, about two miles away. At nine thirty, they told him, they would be back with water and food at one in the afternoon. The party was scheduled to end at three, they were to pick him up at two-thirty. It was a hot October day in North Santa Rosa. He was in dog costume and waving a sign for the Animal Rescue Party. By one o'clock, nobody had brought him food or water, he got some at the gas station, at the intersection he was working. At two-thirty, still nobody had showed up, at three, he began to walk back to the shelter. Eddie had been abandoned by the animal rescue People!!! While walking Eddie yelled out aloud, "Why me? I really must be garbage, if this doesn't mean I'm a loser, I don't know what does!!"

He became well known on the streets, as a happy go lucky, generous, kind and loving person. Unusual for these streets and a sign of weakness to most. Along with that, he was considered a loser, a hard luck case that kept trying, only to fail, for whatever reason, again and again. He didn't care but it affected him negatively, in this society, capitalism, any negative label is going to keep one from getting work. None the less, he continued to show and use love as the answer to everything and anything. Nobody else would talk to him, none of his former colleagues, friends or family, except Rafael, Cheryl and one other, Harald Sigurdsson. Eddie spent time in his compound, as it was his sanctuary.

It was Christmas Eve, the first Christmas Eddie would be alone during and on the street. He was feeling suicidal, thinking about his wife and children and the many wonderful Christmas's they spent together. He had no place to go, all he had owned, was in his back pack, which had become like a ball and chain for him. He also had a bicycle that Harald had given him, he wanted to be sure he got it back, before he killed himself. He went by Harald's but found nobody there, he left the bike and headed to the place where he wanted to hang himself but was unable to do it and returned to Harald's, if he wasn't dead, he needed to keep the bike. The next day, Christmas Day, Eddie found out somebody had robbed Harald's place, specifically, the barn where their meth induced version of the tonight show took place. Eddie became a suspect. Eddie doesn't steal or rob from anyone, he was upset to be a suspect. He felt Harald was special to him and he wished he could find out who did this but couldn't even prove his own innocence. He said to Harald, "I love you man! I could never even imagine robbing from you, I don't steal from anyone. I will do whatever you ask to help you find out who did this. I came by last night to leave the bicycle you gave me when mine was stolen, to give it back because I went to kill myself but III couldn't so I came back and got it." Harald, upset to hear Eddie had almost killed himself on Christmas said, Ï know you didn't do it Eddie, I know you wouldn't do something like that. When it comes to killing yourself, it's not something I want to hear about. You keep trying, you will find your place in this life and it's not by that dumpster either. I love you too, man!!" Eddie was tearing, "Thanks, and I will keep trying. Merry Christmas!"

It was Rafael, though, the one person that had every right to distance himself from Eddie but he didn't. Like Harald, he never gave up on Eddie and kept trying to show him the light. Like Harald, Rafael admired Eddie's ability to keep trying. He still assigned him games, he did basketball and baseball and he did some Rec soccer, which was assigned by the rec depts. themselves. Eddie continued to put together some money and accumulate some things, only to have them stolen.

Eddie did have a couple of other random people that would, "help him". For these people helping always came with a price. One friend who "helped" him, lived on a beautiful ranch, with her parents, Anastasia, was her name. Eddie and she got along very well and she would invite him to stay but he felt he always had to provide some sort of payment, usually meth-amphetamine and he would clean her house, also. He would get tired of becoming like a slave and would leave but always on good terms. He liked it a lot on the ranch, they raised Arabian horses and it was a sprawling property, with lot's to do. Eddie thought he could work there but was never given a chance. While Anastacia proved to be somewhat less of a good friend. Easy to find when Eddie had money but never seen when she had money.

Then there was Jason and Carmen, a couple Eddie knew from the casino, he had hustled some pill deals with Jason and they became friends. Jason asked him to stay with them but it became the same, if not worse than being at Anastasia's ranch. They took care of a woman, who was ninety nine years old but lucid and Eddie would chat with her. They would talk about things that fascinated him, historical times, like the great depression, He would ask her questions and she loved to answer them. He even told her about his children and how upset he was about him and his son not speaking. She told him about his son Frank, "He will learn." Eddie knew that but didn't want his son to learn that way, it probably being the hard way. This house was the most dysfunctional, chaotic place Eddie had ever lived. The give and take was a on a one way street. Eddie is all about fair, he would refrain from staying overnight, for too many reasons to not even visit. He left on good terms but had no plans on visiting again

He also had a friend, Deborah, he had met her at the internet café and would see her at the casino. She had a steady boyfriend, they were just friends, and she was acquainted with the streets but lived in a home. She got him a job working as a phone operator for a phone answering service. He had gotten through the training and he was establishing himself with the company. After working with them for two months, Eddie's friend, Deborah, who got him the job, also had a friend, Toby, where he could rent a room at his house. A very nice house in a very nice suburban neighborhood. Eddie hung out at the house with Toby, they played music together and seemed to get along well but they hadn't known each other that long. Eddie had asked around about the house and his new landlord and didn't hear anything bad. He paid Toby for rent and went grocery shopping and he told him, when he got to the house with the food, "Feel free to eat anything, it's for us." On the third day of Eddie's residency at this house, he came home to a dead man on the couch. Eddie's new Roommate/Landlord, Toby, appeared disheveled and confused and said, "Eddie, I think this guy had a heart attack? He just started making these sounds and it looked like he was having a nightmare, his eyes were closed, then nothing. Can you check and see if he's ok?" Eddie was having one of those, is this really happening moments and offered this help, "I can check but I've never been trained, let me see." Eddie held the man's wrist and checked for a pulse but didn't feel one. He then checked the jugular in the man's neck, nothing there either.

Eddie felt over the man's heart and noticed he wasn't cold and said, "He's still warm, if he's alive but I don't feel any heart beat or pulse anywhere. How long ago did this happen?" Toby wasn't sure, at least that's what he said. Eddie said, "Toby, you have to call 911 now." Toby looked concerned and said, "Yea, I need you to help me, we were going to drive him to the hospital but I can't find my keys. Can you make it across the crawl space to my room, I think the keys are in there?"" Eddie had to find the ladder and after twenty minutes he came out of the room with the keys. When he gave them to

Toby, Toby had his hands filled with garbage and asked Eddie to take the garbage outside. When Eddie returned, he asked, "What is taking this ambulance so long to get here?" Toby still hadn't called 911. Eddie was beginning to freak out and explained, "I'm calling 911 now." Toby said, "No, I got this, we will drive now. I need you to throw out this garbage but not here, go to a store or something." Eddie threw out the garbage but he was worried about the man, who was finally taken to the hospital. He didn't know what was going on before he got there or how long the man had been in the state he was in. When Toby returned, he told Eddie the man had a heart attack and was DOA.

Three days later, Eddie arrived at the house, with Deborah and some groceries but Toby began fighting with Deborah. Eddie didn't know what it was about and brought all the groceries in the house, when on his last trip, he realized his phone was in Deborah's car. As he headed for the car, Toby said to him, "Why didn't you guys come when I called?" Eddie didn't know what he was talking about and Toby said, "I could be leaving and be out all night, you would be locked out." Toby hadn't made Eddie a key and would leave the back door open but since the "heart attack", he was paranoid and didn't want to leave the door open for Eddie. Eddie said, ""Oh well, make the other key and we won't have a problem." With that, Toby closed the door and got into the car driving away and saying "Look see, now you are locked out." Eddie didn't know what to do, the groceries he had just got were not put away and some were perishable. He thought Toby was just fucking with him, when a cop pulled up to the house. The cop said, "We got a call about people fighting, is everything all right?" Eddie told the cop, "Yea, they were fighting but they left. I just moved in here six days ago, I'm not sure about living here, to be honest with you. Some guy had a heart attack three days ago." The cop said, "Heart attack that was no heart attack, that guy overdosed on heroin." Eddie said, "Holy shit, they lied to me and he locked me out." The cop said," If I were you I would get my things and get out of there." Eddie kicked the door in and got his stuff. He knew where to go, the dumpster. It had been becoming abundantly obvious that he was directed to the dumpster and he was meant to stay there. When he spoke to Deborah about getting his phone back, she took Toby's side and got her friend, the manager at the answering service to get rid of him, just as fast as she got him the job, he was out. He thought he had no choice and had to kick in the door, get his things and get out. He certainly didn't think this had anything to do with his job but Deborah was siding with Toby, who was angry about the door. Eddie thought he shouldn't have locked him out on purpose. None the less, Toby threatened to kill Eddie, who had just lost his phone, job and home. He was afraid and had no place to go, he went to the mattress store and slept next to the dumpster, where he felt safe.

Then came the wild fires and suddenly the homeless population doubled, overnight. As Eddie woke up, by the dumpster, and he could smell fire and see smoke. The sounds of fire engines and sirens blaring. Ben arrived at the store, "Eddie, what are you doing here, don't you know what's happening, there's a huge fire in North Santa Rosa, and you got to get out of here. The store is closed until further notice," Eddie scrambled to get his back pack and un-locked his bike and head south to get more information.

The fire had turned to the east, away from the rest of Santa Rosa but most of the northern part of the city was gone. The Red Cross had set up shelter and other services at the fairgrounds. People were everywhere, dazed and confused, some just wandering around, aimlessly. This was nothing like he had ever seen. The fair grounds were not helpful to any homeless people. They tried to sort out the homeless immediately, asking for addresses. Many homeless had camps that were burned but were not able to get help. Eddie was outraged with the homeless segregation taking place, he went to the fairgrounds, and he saw people getting denied, homeless people. He spoke up," What do you think you are doing? These people need help also, just because they didn't own a home, doesn't mean they haven't lost everything, aren't hungry and don't need help." He continued to protest, "Have you lost your collective minds?" Many homeless also help out businesses and receive certain perks, even though they don't actually work on the books for them. They had lost those helpful places and those perks, if the business was affected by fire. The people, red cross volunteers and army national guard, at the fairgrounds seemed to think homeless people were unaffected by the fires and there for freebies and shouldn't be helped.

A woman suffering from obvious psychosis was by a homeless camp, Eddie had joined the people there to see if they needed help. The woman was yelling and cursing at imaginary people, "I don't care who the fuck you are." She had yelled towards nobody.
Eddie tried to make eye contact and speak, "Are you hungry? What is your name? Do you know where your home is?" She said, "Rebeca," She was beginning to understand me, I asked her, "Would you come with me to the Fairgrounds?" She said yes and Eddie put his arm around her, they were right down the street. They got there and Eddie asked Rebeca, "Do you want to speak to a Dr", she was afraid of something and said no. Eddie didn't force the issue but ate with her and she seemed to become more coherent. They returned to the camp and she began again to exercise psychotic behavior and it was a full blown Psychotic episode. Eddie was fascinated, he wanted to help her and was trying to figure out what was going on in her head. Two people approached and were talking to other people when she yelled out, "Who the fuck do you think you

are, Asshole?" The people who had just arrived, Eddie tried to tell them she was sick and before he could get a word out, the woman punched Rebeca. She was stunned but didn't even seem to realize she had been hit. Eddie said, "I was just trying to tell you she's not well." The woman offered no apology or seemed to care at all. "Rebeca", Eddie said, "Are you Ok, let's walk back to the fairgrounds." He took her to the medical tent and explained what happened and how she was behaving, also. He saw her days later, bruised badly and still not well. She was with someone and he didn't want to interfere. After things began to settle down and get a little more normal for the city, the thing that got worse, the number of homeless people that had doubled stayed the same. He continued to try to save and make efforts to get off the street.

He got another part time job, with a caterer. He also started to do the breathing exercises and meditation he had learned years ago in grief counseling. He was trying not to self-medicate and use alternatives to deal with the emotions and feelings concerning his children, Christina and Frank that he loved and missed so much. Several months went by and nothing changed, except the things he had to replace that were continual stolen.

Eddie had to officiate basketball, a day after working 14 hours for the caterer. He had no place to go that night and stayed up. Still trying to refrain from drug use and still using meditation and breathing to cope with his emotions. Exhausted, he arrived at the gym early to Officiate and he feel asleep outside the gym, they couldn't wake him. He had screwed Rafael, who had assigned him the games.

Then came the end of Eddie's sanctuary, Harald Sigurdsson's compound was being sold and Harald had to move. The late night chemically unbalanced talk show that Eddie loved was being cancelled. He no longer had a special place to go, where he could forget about life for a while, find peace, solitude and a helping hand. He helped Harald at the compound and said goodbye to his sanctuary.

He couldn't live like this anymore. He was spinning his wheels, until it hit him, after five years. He had to find home, where his heart is. He didn't have any ruby slippers to click the heels together and say, there's no place like home and he didn't know where home was or how to get there. He was still dreaming, sleeping next to the dumpster.

He woke up from the dream, which was his reality, by the mattress store, he had to set up the outdoor display for Fourth of July weekend. He had fallen asleep hoping, as he always did, that he would wake up and it was all a nightmare but it was real and he was still homeless.

He planned that he would work the weekend and use the money to get back east, to be near his children. That was what was important, nothing else mattered. All the love he shared on these streets, all the shirts off his back, returned wallets, all he is and all he gave was love, it was all he had. He had to get home but he had to find out where that was.

Chapter 11

Can't Find My Way Home

Eddie thought he knew what he had to do, find home, he thought it had to be near his children, geographically. More importantly, his children were where his heart is, he would let his love for them guide him, to be close to them, even if they didn't want him, it was what he felt he had to do. He finished the weekends work but he didn't know where to start with his solution to get home. He spent the money on a motel room over the next week. The next week, someone at 600 Morgan Street, the Catholic Charities Homeless Service Center, had told him that they can provide transportation. He sought out a worker there and sure enough, if he had someone on the other end of the destination, they would get him there. He asked his friends on Facebook, if they would be able to help him by providing a place for a short time. A woman, he had previously had a short lived relationship with agreed but he had to take with him some marijuana for her. He figured he would bring more than what she wanted and sell it to old friends, so he would have some money to live on. He went to Harald's, to get some weed, for himself, the woman he was going to stay with and to sell. He also got some meth for the trip. He was saying goodbye to his good friend again and he knew he would miss him but as usual, when he is leaving any place, nobody knows if he will return. Even Eddie never knows whether he will be back again or not, it seems nothing is permanent in his life and anything is possible for the happy go lucky, free spirited person, he had become.

He went to the mattress store, and said good bye to Glen and CA, again, for what he was thinking would be the last time. Once again, he had given his all, he never stopped doing the right thing, even when he was starving and broke, and he loved one another. He had tried his best to get out of the situation he was in. He prayed to God to help and guide him. Now it was "U2, Walk On", playing in his head. He felt he had a purpose, his daughter was 16 and Eddie was concerned she might rebel in her extremist catholic home and try to come find him. It was a dangerous prospect, if she had it and Eddie wanted to make sure it didn't happen. So, Eddie walked on, all the love, kindness and help he had been giving on the streets, all he had learned, he was walking on with it. Eddie boarded a one-way Greyhound to NJ. Music once again played in his head, "And love is not the easy thing, the only baggage that you can bring. Love is not the easy thing, the only baggage you can bring is all that you can't leave behind." He thought of his children, Christina and Frank and how they were kept apart from each other. The music played on, "And if the darkness is to keep us apart and if the daylight feels like it's a long way off and if your glass heart should crack and for a second you turn back. Oh no, be strong, Walk on. Walk on. What you got, they can't steal it, and no they can't even feel it. Walk on. Walk on. Stay safe tonight. You're packing a suitcase for a place, none of us has been. A place that has to be believed, to be seen. You could have flown away, a singing bird, in an open cage, who will only fly, only fly for freedom. Walk on. Walk on. What you got they can't deny it, can't sell it or buy it Walk on. Walk on, stay safe tonight and I know it aches, how your heart it breaks and you can only take so much, walk on, walk on." Eddie knew where he was going, it was where his heart was. "Home, hard to know what it is, if you never had one. Home, I can't say where it is but I know I'm going home, it's where the heart is."

Eddie had his children's pictures on his lap the whole ride, he cried and thought of what he would say to them, when he got there. He phoned Fran, Christina's adoptive mom and left a message that he was coming and that he needed to see Christina. He felt alive, sober again, with a purpose. He felt his soul had returned, he felt whole again. He didn't know what he was doing or how to go about it but he knew he had to be there, by his children.

Eddie's friend was picking him up at the bus station, in NJ. He got to NJ, she met him, he had to see a friend about the weed he wanted to sell, and she drove him there but then ditched him there. Eddie had more weed coming and it was being sent to her house in two days. She tried to rob it but he got to the sender just in time and cancelled the shipment.. Now he was without a place to go, he had the weed he came with and went to his old park, where he hung out as a kid and played ball with his son. As he neared the park, a police officer slowed down to look at him, he thought nothing of it. He went to the park and smoked, as he tried to think about what he was going to do. Suddenly head lights appeared at the park entrance, it was the police, followed by three more police cars. Eddie had finished smoking, they approached him and asked him about his daughter. Fran had called them and gave them unsubstantiated warnings about him. Eddie came in peace, as he always does, he was filled with love and all he wanted to do was see his children, especially, his daughter. His phone call to his daughter's adoptive parents was respectful, he simply wanted to see his daughter. He had concerns about her, not knowing what could go through the head of a sixteen year old young woman. Considering, this was a sixteen year old who had lost her mom when she was four and was taken away from her dad six months later. He was afraid she might want to try and find him and he wanted a line of communication open for her, for whatever questions she might have.

They said, "Don't go to your daughter's house. "Eddie barked back, "Who are you to tell me whether or not to go to my daughter's house?" With that they said, "We smell pot, give us your bag." Eddie had to give it up and Eddie threw it on the ground. Next thing Eddie knew, he was in in handcuffs. This was not the home coming he was expecting?

It got worse. The next day, after reacting unkindly to someone on Facebook, for their questioning of Eddie's integrity concerning his daughter, the police, once again came to harass him. He was kicked, thrown to the ground and shackled. They took him to a mental hospital. He came in peace and filled with love, they released him a few days later. Now he was homeless in the place he grew up and he was facing charges for marijuana. How could he explain this or anything to his children? Eddie now had to stay in NJ for the charge, his son won't answer his calls and they won't let him see his daughter. Eddie came in peace, full of love and with righteous intent, only to be beaten and kept from his purpose, to find home, where his heart is. He thought he knew where his heart was, even if he didn't know where home was. His peace was confronted with hatred, his good met evil. Distraught, he went to the baseball field, where he played as a child and coached his son as an adult and volunteered hundreds of hours. He took down the flag from center field, for the rope. He left the flag on the ground and walked to the backstop behind home plate. He climbed and tied the rope at the top. He lay on the fencing, at the top of the back stop, to the front pole, tied the rope to, now the other end around his neck. He looked down and thought of his son Frank, how he taught him so much here, not just baseball and the moments but about life, love and happiness. He thought about the moments he also had here as a child. He began to cry uncontrollably, he had come back here for this? To hang himself on this field, where he had so many great moments?

He cried out to God, "Why is this happening to me, what do I have to do?" He was hungry, tired, beat up and once again completely heart broken. "Why God? I do the right thing, I come in peace, and I'm filled with love."

Even though Frank wouldn't speak to him, he couldn't do it, he promised him he wouldn't and he climbed back down.

Eddie was telling a complete stranger the recent events he had been through. The Stranger told him to write it down and he thought, "That's it, I need to write the whole story. So, my kids will know, so other people will see and they might not be so quick to judge anyone. Maybe they could learn something from this story."

Eddie had no resources in NJ, he had nothing, for the next two months, he went to the library every day to write. There was a time limit, if someone was waiting to use a computer, he would have to give up his. At night, he went to the mall, he pitched a tent between the mall and the library. Both his children lived within a mile of where he had his tent. He walked by the homes they lived in, hoping to see them. His daughter lived adjacent to a park, where he would sit on a bench and try to get a glimpse of Christina, who was once Daddy's Girl, to her and still was to him, he would sit there and cry. At the mall, he would think, if he saw her, he would know and he looked for her in the crowded mall. Then, while walking by the house Christina lived in, the adoptive father was outside, Eddie approached him, he was crying, he was soaking himself with his tears. He said, "I want to see Christina, talk to her, I need to know how she is, I need to let her know that I love her and miss her more than she will ever know." Christina's adoptive father stopped Eddie and said, "Please, she's not even here." Eddie interjected, "Please? Did you say, please? I'm the one saying please and on my daughter's behalf, as well. There can never be any good in keeping us apart." Christina's adoptive father, Dick, said, "She's doing fine, don't worry." Eddie replied in factually, "I'm her father, she's my girl, "don't worry"? I will always worry. The fact that you don't understand that worries me more as her adoptive father. She was taken from me, I didn't give her up, and I fought to keep her."

Eddie prayed for guidance from above. The directions he was given have led him to a dangerous destination, filled with pain and suffering along the way. He needed spiritual guidance, from a higher level. He asked his wife, his dad and god to guide him. He had remained in the light this far but this light he was seeking was a different kind of light, this was an ultra violet or divine light. He screamed aloud, "I can't live, I give up, give me guidance!" and he began to write. As another song filled his head. "Ultraviolet", "Sometimes I feel like I don't know, sometimes I feel like checkin' out. I want to get it wrong, can't always be strong and love it won't be long. Oh sugar, don't you cry, oh child, wipe the tears from your eyes. You know I need you to be strong and the day is as dark as the night is long. Feel like trash, you make me feel clean, I'm in the black, can't see or be seen. Baby, baby, baby...light my way. You bury your treasure where it can't be found but your love is like a secret that's been passed around. There is a silence that comes to a house, where no one can sleep. I guess it's the price of love, I know it's not cheap. Baby, baby, baby...light my way. Ultraviolet. I remember when we could sleep on stones. Now we lie together, in whispers and moans. When I was all messed up and I had opera in my head, your love was a light bulb hanging over my bed. Baby, baby, baby...light my way."

The song played on in his head, as loud as ever and he wrote and kept writing this story, he had thought about it before. He knows the content is interesting and he had some wild experiences to write about. He reflected on the past ten years, they are filled with ups and downs, a roller coaster of good times and bad. After all, he knows what it was like to be Adam and Eve and even bit the apple, surely someone can learn from that. Mostly, he thought about how people have defined him because of his situation. A situation that when people find themselves in, they wonder how they got there and usually come up empty. Eddie's been figuring out how and it wasn't all his fault, in fact he was directed here by someone very close to him, someone he believed in and was taught to trust that they wanted the best for him but this person didn't, it was his own mother and family. Then there were mistakes that people made that ruined his reputation and had him lose jobs. There were lots of bad things that happen to him, a good person. Why should he bare sole responsibility, while others go without accountability and receive no validation?

People should know that nobody wants to be in this situation and they don't get there by themselves, he felt he had the experiences to prove it. He tried to do the right thing and address concerns with his peers and he was fired and black listed because they feared they would be removed, since those concerns were their responsibility. He was doing the right thing, as he always did. He worked, he gave back to his community, what did he do to deserve being in this situation but to the hierarchy, he was a threat. He had to share this story, he had to write it to right the tide against him because the judgement was wrong and he did the right thing. He thought, mostly, he had to get the story to his kids, he had to have it explained to them, so they could see, and he's a righteous man. Hungry, again, he asked God for help and he provides, yet again but why?

Eddie begin to realize that the love and support he desires from his family and friends is not coming but God's love and support has always been there for him. God is the one and only and Gods love and support is all he thinks he needs. God keeps him going and more, he inspires him to not give up. After all, God hasn't given up on him, he still gives him love and support. Eddie wants the story to be read by those that judge and define the people of the streets. So, they might see, it's next to impossible to get out of their situation. He had to write it, it's all he has got, love. Love for one another.

He waits, looks for signs, directions and spreads the love that fills his heart. He waits for the light to take away this darkness that keeps his children and him apart. He waits and he loves one another. He has faith that God's Love will guide them all and bring them all back together. He believes God has all the love and support he needs to survive and help him tell this story. He looks for the directions that will lead him to Happy Street. Eventually, he will bring his family back together and he will be home again, in his heart, where his home is, on Happy Street, filled with peace and love. For now, he can't find his way home and that song was all he could hear.

"Come down off your throne and leave your body alone. Somebody must change. You are the reason I've been waiting so long. Somebody holds the key.

But I'm near the end and I just ain't got the time And I'm wasted and I can't find my way home. Come down on your own and leave your body alone. Somebody must change.
You are the reason I've been waiting all these years. Somebody holds the key. But I can't find my way home."

With his book complete, Eddie sends out the manuscript to every Publisher and Literary Agent he could find. In the meantime, his court case in NJ has been adjourned, marijuana is about to be made legal in NJ and the charge against him dismissed, he is free to leave NJ but the case remained open. He came in peace, he tried again to address a problem with a solution made from a recipe of love. Alone again, on a deserted island, he deals with the rejection his love received. It will have to wait some more and he must survive.

In the night time, while at the mall in NJ, Eddie is tuned in to politics on TV, he watches in the mall lounge, he is intrigued. With the current administration in the White House, he has been feeling the need for him to return to politics. Eddie is a progressive democrat, maybe a socialist and feels the President is a dangerous person to run the USA, both here and abroad, the world is losing any respect they had for the USA. Where he lives, the San Francisco North Bay, as well as other regions in CA, there have been wildfires. The President has been extremely insensitive to Californians, blaming the state's governor for fires that are on federal land.

Eddie has been paying attention to the upcoming midterm elections and several Candidates have given him reason to want to work for them. He contacts the Richard Ortega for Congress Campaign, it's the third congressional district in West Virginia. He speaks to a Field Office Manager, Tanya Briggs and explains, "I would like to be a part of the campaign. I like this Candidates agenda and platform but mostly this district is the most challenging long shot possibility in the country." The woman asked him to send a resume, he did and she called him back saying, "Mr. Campagnola, we have a position for you." Eddie was thrilled and asked about accommodations, "If you can find me a place to stay, I would be happy with that, food and transportation costs and we would be square." She replied, I have you as a hired payed employee, and we can get you a place to stay too."

Eddie is going to keep trying, keep living, keep surviving and wait for his children to hear and know his story, so they might know what has happened to him, how much he loves them and misses them. This is what Eddie does, he keeps trying, and he gets knocked down and gets up again, fails but keeps trying. It's a greyhound bus, destination, Bluefield, West Virginia and the third congressional district campaign.

It was five weeks until the election, when Eddie joined the campaign to elect Richard Ortegaa to congress. The Bluefield, WV 3rd district field office Manager, Tanya Briggs, met him at the bus stop. She was a thirty-one year old West Virginian lifer but probably would accept an opportunity to live and work elsewhere. This campaign could get her an offer to work in Washington DC, if Ortega got elected, as a staffer, a victory could mean the same for anyone who worked the campaign.

For his accommodations, he was given an air mattress and a section in the office to sleep. The office was a union headquarters and it had a kitchen also. These were the best accommodations he had in some time.

Without any drugs or vices for three months, no bicycle or officiating Eddie's slim athletic build had changed. He left CA, in great shape at 146 lbs. He was now 158 lbs. and completely out of shape. He was hired by the campaign to do several things, one of which was to field canvas and field canvasing in West Virginia means all hills. It would be hard for him at first but by the second week, he was briskly hiking up and down the hills of West Virginia.

He was out of the cave he had been living in for the past six years, he wasn't isolated anymore and he was working well with others. In the office, there were Tanya, Tiffany, Brian and two interns, Sam and Gail. He was enjoying being a go to guy once again, he was the elder statesman in the office, experienced and wise. He spent a lot of time talking with Tanya and she shared everything with him, he listened, advised and she would implement his thoughts into the offices operations. He thrived in this environment, he was beginning to feel much better about himself. He hadn't worked on a campaign for A Candidate in twenty-five years but explained to Tanya, "I have never lost a campaign I worked on." Tanya was in disbelief, "Never lost." she said. Eddie corrected himself," Well I worked on legislative campaigns that lost but I never worked on an election for a candidate that lost. So, we can't loss".

Tanya showed Eddie around the region, the third district of West Virginia, the southern portion. An area with rugged mountainous terrain, more rugged than anywhere else east of the Mississippi and the most scenic and beautiful state that side as well. Eddie had his thoughts on West Virginia's future he shared with Tanya, "West Virginia, it's so beautiful but I have never seen any tourism advertisements. You all need to diversify and move on when it comes to the history, when it comes to outsiders coming here, using the people, taking the natural resources and leaving an environmental mess. I would definitely have a shit load of windmills on these ridges, all over these mountains, like Nevada and CA." Eddie had become cynical when it came to our societies and humanities treatment of each other. He felt the divisive agenda of the political parties needed to end and the Democratic Party, specifically, needed to return to its past platforms. To him, the labor movement and the blue collar support the Democrats had depended on had been abandoned by the party and were either voting for someone else or not voting at all. He wanted to support Progressive Democrats that wanted to return the Democratic Party to its old self, with the progressive agenda, concerning the environment and social issues, like legal marijuana.

He felt, globally, the USA is the only country that is preventing any globalization because we are too greedy and selfish. Eddie would share with the interns and Tanya, "It's inevitable that globalization will take place. Like with climate change, we can't ignore this stuff, we have to accept this and then we can start a transition, slowly. President Trump, building walls, Mr. President, remember Reagan to Gorbachev, tear down this wall? It's just, what could be more divisive than a wall, which by the way, you can go over, around or under." Eddie feared that the President wanted to be a Dictator, "He's going to manipulate or manufacture a state of emergency, then, since he has the most pro presidential Supreme Court, they will vote to give him supreme power during this state of emergency, which will never end." He wanted to empower and create a sense of urgency among his fellow campaign workers and volunteers, to get them psyched he would say, "This is our last chance, it's the final nail in the coffin if we don't win the majority in Congress back, this midterm election." He hated fear mongering but he was doing it, he thought maybe we should be afraid of our President if his intentions were to become a Dictator. He also shared his sense of humor, whenever it was appropriate, especially with the two interns, Sam and Gail. Eddie always connected well with young people their age. He would mock their Candidate's opponent constantly, mostly for refusing to debate the issues. He also did an impression of the Candidate they were working for, Richard Ortega, he tried to make work fun and he did. They made up a game during phone canvasing, a version of bingo and he would blurt out Bingo and try to use each square, connected or not to claim victory.

The office phone canvased, field canvased and did polling, eventually, it was time to get out the vote. This meant getting back to the people they know are supporters and do whatever they can to get them to the poles and vote.

Eddie had gotten back into politics and was feeling empowered by the work. In the office he began to feel important again, to others, he loved being a go to guy. When he had a house of six and was maintaining, scheduling and mostly fixing problems anyone had, he thrived, it made him happy, and working on the campaign offered the same feelings. Eddie was getting the much needed directions to some place other than a dumpster, they were the directions back home. The sort of directions he hadn't gotten in twelve years, since his wife passed away. He was letting God do the driving for him and it was working. He was working in an office, with a computer and interns and living with decent accommodations, he hadn't had any of these things for a long time.

His mind still unavoidably reviewing the visuals stored in his brain when triggered, he would see them less and cry less. While using the methods he learned over the years, to reduce the episodes of emotional breakdowns that leave him emotionally paralyzed. Here in WV, working on this campaign, he was kept busy and had less time to allow for random thoughts to trigger any emotional paralysis.

The office often had open discussions during training periods, Eddie wasn't shy about sharing his points of view. During a discussion on equality, Eddie said, "I live as if "Imagine", the lyrics, were reality. I can't wait for "Imagine" to actually become reality, and since it doesn't look like it will happen during my time, I have no choice."

The campaign, which started out behind by forty points, had gained momentum and with a week before the election, was trailing in the polls by only ten points. The field canvas had stepped up its efforts and Eddie was phone canvasing after his field canvas hours, as well. One week before the election and Eddie got a contract offer from a publisher to publish his manuscript. The offer did not include an advance but it wasn't going to cost him anything. He didn't want to wait for other offers, he copied and signed the contract. The publishing company then sent him a couple of requests of their own. He had to help out with the sales materials and the wording on them. He also needed to give them a cover design.

This last week of the campaign would be the busiest time, while they focused on get out the vote. Eddie would have no time to satisfy the publishing company's requests, until after the election.
Eddie had to go someplace, he had to buy a bus ticket, and he really didn't know where to go. He loved West Virginia but the locals were having a hard time finding employment and as he searched for a job, like the people of WV, he couldn't find anything.
He had left CA without completing a program for first offenders. He had been charged with misdemeanor weapon possession, brass knuckles, which were lying next to him while he slept in a park. The police were allegedly on foot patrol when they found Eddie, they charged him with the weapon. In order to avoid court, Eddie took the program option for first offenders. He also felt the book was written about being homeless in CA and that would be the best place to begin the marketing and promotion to sell the book.
He decided he was going to go back to CA and he also arranged to return to the mattress store and work the Veterans Day weekend, as the sign waver. To get there in time to work, he would have to leave Election night and not attend the victory party, which he had a feeling wasn't going to happen anyway.

The time had come, it was election night and Eddie was preparing to leave for CA, on the Greyhound bus, which left at seven-thirty on Tuesday night, November sixth. He had to board his bus to CA, he had worked hard, right to the last minute, and everyone on the campaign deserved a pat on the back.

This was a challenging race but Eddie knew, they were going to come up a little bit short of victory and he wouldn't be missing any victory party. The two interns, he had become friendly with, had volunteered to take him to the bus station and say good-bye. He had spoken to them about his son Frank, since they were close in age to him, he thought they might be able to give him advice. They had tried their best to help him but his son still wouldn't reply to any of his attempts to communicate with him. He asked them to try to connect with his son on Facebook and let him know that they were interns, who worked with his dad, on the campaign. He asked them to explain to his son what he, his dad, was going through and how much he spoke about him, so he might know how his dad was doing. At the bus stop, Eddie thanked them for the ride and for the work they did on the campaign. They gave him a thank you card and they all said good bye and they gave each other hugs.

Chapter 12

The Dumpster is Home

Eddie boarded the bus for CA, he would check on his phone for the election results. He had a five hour wait in

Columbus, Ohio, he read the thank you letter from the interns.

"Dear Eddie, Thank you for being you, and for being the funniest and coolest person in the office. You are one of the most caring, passionate and exciting people I have ever met. You have made our internship one of the best experiences of our lives and it was an honor to get to know you. From our daily political discussions, funny comments, about Carol Mills, random jokes and stories about phone calls and canvasing. No matter how hard you try, you will never cheat your way to winning Phone Banking Bingo. We hope you have safe travels back to California, and we hope you and your son work things out. We will miss you greatly, and you better stay in touch. Best wishes, Sam and Gail."

Eddie was crying, as he folded up the thank you note and placed it back into the envelope. He knew he had connected with them, in a father, sort of statesman way but he didn't think or believe that anyone had ever thought so highly of him. Eddie was getting directions home, away from the dumpster and he had begun to feel very good about himself. Something he hadn't felt in years, since his wife had passed, twelve years ago. During the time he spent on this campaign, he was looked up to and shown an enormous amount of respect. He felt important again, he was the go to guy, he was empowered by all of this and he was excited about getting back to working on marketing and promoting his book. The publisher had requested a couple things, a cover design, some marketing literature and the tittle he had chosen, was taken and he needed a new one. Originally titled, "Going to California", he had come up with, "Directions to the Dumpster" or "Can't Find My Way Home" and he wasn't sure which to use.

Eddie hadn't slept for thirty hours, as the bus entered Kansas, he finally fell asleep. He was awakened by the passenger next to him, Carl. He and Carl had lunch the day before at a White castle in Indianapolis. Carl was on his way to a funeral in Washington, he and Eddie befriended each other and sat next to each when they boarded the bus. They were at the Kansas, Colorado boarded, and the bus was making an hour long stop. Eddie and Carl got some breakfast, both were feeling good after some sleep and something to eat. They board the bus and Carl had his phone, he was showing Eddie some things. They weren't being loud, mostly just watching the video's each of them were selecting. Eddie had spoken to Carl the day before about the election and that they had lost the race. They were watching cartoons now and Carl asked Eddie, "Have you ever seen the cartoons where characters like, Bugs Bunny and Road Runner get killed?" Eddie was surprised and said, "No, you mean they don't trick, "Elmer Fud" and "Wil E. Coyote"?" Carl said, "Exactly, you got to see this, it's so funny." They began to watch, after "Wil E Coyote" caught "The road Runner", he was on the dining room table, like a Thanksgiving dinner. The passenger sitting in the row in front of Eddie and Carl, slowly and deliberately, he turned towards them, as to not alert them, his arm had raised to the top of the back of his seat, as he faced Eddie. Not thinking anything of it, Eddie watched the video, when suddenly, the man lunged toward Eddie, in his hand, an eight inch flat head screw driver. The weapon penetrated Eddie's left upper cheek, scrapped his upper, then lower teeth and gums, continuing down his throat, finishing deep in the back of his throat and damaging the artery. He pulled it out and struck again, this time a half inch above Eddie's right eye. The Attacker was screaming, "Shut the fuck up. Shut the fuck up!!"Eddie went into shock, his brain had turned his body off, he didn't feel anything, and he was dazed and confused. He ended up in the isle, as Carl stood up and grabbed the attacker, he was struck also, his left ear cut in half.

Carl grabbed the man's arms and body, constricting him this time and he began to softly and slowly talk to the attacker. "Everything is going to be alright, you are ok. Nobody is going to hurt you, you can sit back down." The attacker listened to Carl and sat back down, against the window, on his heels and he lit a cigarette. The bus had stopped and the other passengers were yelling at the Attacker, to get off the bus and he did. As, Carl, who had just saved Eddie's life and possibly others on the bus, attended to Eddie, who was on the floor in the isle, crawling towards the back of the bus. Carl kneeled down by Eddie and said, "Are you alright, let me see your face." Eddie turned to look at Carl, as blood came out of his mouth and said, "My mouth is filling with blood, I don't know what I should do, let it come out or swallow it?" Eddie's brain was returning his body functions back to normal but he still wasn't sure about what had just happened. Carl told him, "Spit it out, you are bleeding a lot and that's what I can see, you got cut more internally, in your throat. Don't worry, I'm here, we will get you fixed up." Eddie noticed Carl's ear and said, "Man, your ear is cut in half, what the fuck just happened?" Carl said, "Don't worry, somebody just flipped out and started stabbing at us, I stopped him and he is off the bus now, we are safe." A woman, with a baby had wipes for Eddie and Carl and Carl gave a few to Eddie and said, "Here, take this and apply pressure to the cut above your right eye." Carl did the same to his ear. The bus was in the middle of nowhere, just across the Kansas border into Colorado. The assailant waited outside the bus for police, while Eddie and Carl waited for an ambulance. Eddie was bleeding a lot and his mouth kept filling up with blood but he remained coherent. For Eddie, time was a concern, the first strike had hit and damaged the artery in his throat. He hadn't passed out and noticed that if he held his head a certain way, the bleeding slowed down. Finally the police arrived and immediately took the assailant into custody. Then the ambulance arrived, Carl helped

Eddie off the bus and into the ambulance. He said to Eddie, "I got to get back on the bus, I have a warrant in NY and I will get arrested if the police run my name." Eddie told Carl, "You have to go to the hospital, your ear is hanging on your head, and you have to see it to believe it." The ambulance driver had a mirror and gave it to Carl, who looked at himself and said. "Yea, I guess you are right, if I want my ear, I have to stay in this ambulance." The police did exactly what Carl thought they would and they told him to get out of the ambulance, so they could arrest him. Eddie spoke up, with blood coming out of his mouth with each word "Officer, he needs to go to the hospital, this man just saved my life and maybe others on this bus. He single handedly stopped this maniac, while the man cut half his ear off." Carl told Eddie, who was visibly having trouble speaking, "Eddie, try not to speak, it's making your throat bleed more." The ambulance driver then said, "It's ok with us if he comes, we don't have time to talk about it, this guy needs help fast." Referring to Eddie's throat and the amount of blood he was losing. The police said ok and they sped off to the hospital. Eddie wanted to ask Carl about the attack but couldn't speak anymore. Carl told the EMT's what had happened and Eddie listened, there wasn't really much to it, the passenger in front of them just turned and started to stab Eddie. Eddie had completely gone into shock but now he was getting back to functioning somewhat normally. At the local hospital, Eddie was stitched and Carl got his ear put back together but Eddie's throat needed a specialist. Eddie was taken to Swedish hospital, outside Denver CO. Carl had to be taken to county jail, he was going to the same place his attacker, whom he had stopped from killing Eddie and possibly others on the bus.

Eddie saw Carl, as they were both leaving the hospital, he thanked Carl, "Carl, I don't know what to say? Holy shit!" Carl stopped him, "Don't say anything, your throat

is fucked up enough, I know, I know, we will be ok."
Eddie didn't care and had to tell Carl, "You saved my life, man. I don't know why and you risked your own for me and had your ear cut in half doing it. I owe you, thank you, you are an amazing man. It's unbelievable that you are going to jail, after what you just did, thank you!" Carl said, "No worries. The warrant was old and although it was a felony, most of the charges will be dismissed. I will be fine but I don't think I will make the funeral, I hate those things anyway." Eddie agreed, "Me too. I got to go and try to avoid my own funeral, my throat is still bleeding." Carl was escorted by Police, in handcuffs. Hard to imagine, a selfless Hero, that nobody will know about, except Eddie, being taken to jail.

Before leaving for Denver, a victims advocate from Colorado's "Victims Compensation" program, introduced herself to Eddie. Her name was Sally and she explained that they would cover all hospital and other costs.

During the ride to Denver, by ambulance, since Eddie had found the position of his head, greatly slowed the bleeding, he tried to recollect what had just happened. His brain had already created the visual, it was permanently loaded into his head, and he was already viewing it, and it kept playing. He had already had a library of these flashback visuals that he was trying to escape from. This one, an attempt on his very own life, a man two feet in front of him, savagely, repeatedly, stabbing him in the face. He couldn't stop the visual or make it go away. The man kept shouting, "Shut the fuck up! Shut the fuck up!" The screw driver plunging into Eddie's face and being pulled out and stuck right back in his face. His attacker continuing, "Shut the fuck up! Shut the fuck up!"

The ambulance arrived at Swedish Hospital, in Englewood, CO, Eddie was admitted and placed in ICU. The throat specialist was on his way, Eddie was consumed with what he couldn't get out of his head. The Doctor arrived and began to examine the artery, he asked Eddie, "How bad is your pain, one, being the least pain and ten being most painful?" Eddie replied, "My throat is a ten, when I try to swallow." The Doctor said, "Then don't swallow." Eddie chuckled, the Doctor said, "I'm glad you are finding humor, that's an old one but good one but I was being serious. I have this tube, like the dentists have." He gave the tube to Eddie, and he placed it in his mouth. The dark red blood filled the tube, as it ran out to the sink, Eddie asked the Doctor, " Is that ok, I've been watching a lot of blood come out of me, I filled almost two bags since the attack? I noticed that when I hold my head in a certain position, it bleeds less, I will try my best to maintain that position." The Doctor said, "I will schedule the surgery and check back soon, definitely position where ever it bleeds less." For a brief moment, Eddie had gotten away from the attack that was repeatedly playing out in his mind. He refused pain medication, he hadn't used anything for five months, and he wanted to stay that way. He couldn't eat or drink anything and he was being fed intravenously. He tried to think of other things, like his family. He wondered if his family, his children would be able to find out what had and was happening to him. He thought that maybe this would create, at least, some dialog between his family and he. What he really wanted was their love and support. His loneliness itself was hard for him but being alone during these life altering events was what hurt him most. He gave the nurse emergency contact information, it was his mom and son and they left messages with both of them.

When the Doctor came for a second visit, his examination of Eddie's throat showed that the bleeding had significantly slowed and he cancelled surgery.

Eddie also noticed that the blood coming out of the tube, had become a much lighter shade of red. By the third day, the bleeding stopped completely. On the fourth day, he was placed in a regular room and was scheduled to be released. He was walking the hall and peeked in some rooms, taking notice of the family and friends, with cards and flowers for the patients that occupied the rooms. He had spent his four days either thinking about the attack or thinking about the absence of his friends and family. The victims advocate bought him a plane ticket to SF, it would be the last thing they would do for him and five days after being savagely attacked, without provocation and after he successfully fought for his life, he was on his way back to CA. Since the attack, Eddie hadn't thought about anything else but the attack and having to go through it all alone. Now, he had to face life, afraid and already suffering with acute PTSD. He hadn't followed up on any of the options he had for his basic needs, he hadn't secured a place to stay in CA. He did call Glen, at the mattress store, to let him know what happened and that he wouldn't be able to work. He ended the conversation by saying, "Didn't I say, I can put myself out there, can get it together, be in a great place personally and something bad always has to ruin it. Now, you've seen it happen a couple times yourself. This last time, somebody tried to kill me! If I try again, it will surely be the end of me. "

Eddie would never be the same person that crossed into Colorado on the morning of November eighth, on a Greyhound bus, that day had changed him forever. He was in a great place when he left WV, empowered and feeling good about himself. He had to go right to work at the mattress store and he was psyched about working with the publisher on the book. Now he had to face the world, a different person, he boarded the plane from Denver to SF, afraid that at any time, any moment, someone could attack him or try to kill him. The experience left him thinking that his fellow man was capable of anything, even attempting to kill him, without provocation, at any moment. He was constantly looking over his shoulder and he kept his distance from everyone.

When he got to Santa Rosa, he rented a motel room and stayed in the motel room, starring at the walls, only leaving to eat. He had to talk himself into getting the door open, then talk himself into actually leaving. He didn't want to communicate with anyone and, as usual, nobody was trying to communicate with him. It was three weeks until his hospital stay follow up visit, with his Doctor in Santa Rosa. That would be the day he would also run out of money and no longer be able to stay at the motel. The day of his Doctor appointment, he also had to go to the court house to take care of a matter there. This was his first journey out in public, other than a short walk down the street to eat and that proved difficult to him. To start his trip, he would have to take a bus, which he was unable to do. He couldn't get the visual of the attack out of his head, on the bus, he became ill, motion sickness, forced him to exit the bus and walk instead. He made it to court and was placed back into the first offender program. He was to call them within three days but when he tried to do it immediately, he couldn't find his phone, it had been stolen.

He then went to his Doctors appointment, where he was given paperwork and referrals for other Doctors. He saw the Psychiatrist, who also gave him referrals and phone numbers. The Doctors were concerned for Eddie's wellbeing and the fact that he simply was unable to function normally at the time. Eddie left the Doctors, with no phone, no money and no place to go and no way to follow up on any Doctors orders.

By email, Eddie contacted the Victims Compensation people from CO, to see what he could be compensated for. He filled out all the paperwork, all he could get were the lost wages and heard nothing. He had the lost wages to be compensated. He finally heard back from them and they chastised him for asking if there was any compensation for pain and suffering. Victim's compensation said that they were not a charity, they actually accused him of looking for a hand out.

They also denied his lost wages claim, since he earned cash, even though he had given them the names of those who would have paid him. As usual for Eddie, and the life altering events he has endured, there would be no compensation, no validation and he would have to go through it all alone, with no love and support. He spoke to Glen, at the store. "Glen, what's the point in trying anymore, anyway. Even if I were to get out of this situation, I have no life, my family hates me, I can't communicate with my children, so for who, for what?" Glen replied, "For you, for yourself, so you can live comfortably." Eddie disagreed, saying, "I can't live without my children, there isn't enough comfort for me to find that could ever make me happy without them. I love them so much and I miss them and they don't even know how much they matter to me, nothing else matters to me. How can it be that something matter so much to me and I matter nothing to them?" Glen came back with the same thing he had been saying, "But you have to keep trying."

The visual in his head kept playing but Eddie began to examine the situation differently, he became paranoid and believed his attacker had a motive. Like the others who had been giving him directions, he thought his attacker was pissed off that he could possibly think he was anything other than garbage and think he could leave the dumpster. For the first time, he began to think that maybe the dumpster was his home, that his heart wasn't where his home was because he didn't have a heart anymore. His heart had been broken so severely, it couldn't be his home, only the dumpster was his home. He had followed the directions he was given and they were the right directions, the directions to the dumpster and he was there. Eddie was looking for answers that nobody could really answer. There had to be some reason for all of this to happen to him, it had to be because he left the dumpster. Because he thought he could do something good and be somebody. Someone attempted to murder him and he felt it was because he was trying to find another home, the one in his heart, with his family and especially his children. He wanted to be important, useful and contribute to society but something, someone was directing him back to the dumpster. This attack was the same message that he had been getting for many years, trying to tell him that he's garbage and direct him to his home, the dumpster. He should go to the dumpster and, like the man said, "Shut the fuck up! Shut the fuck up!"

It was, he thought, maybe, this was an evil conspiracy, that evil wanted to keep him down and stop him from loving one another and keep the darkness that kept him and his children apart.

Now Eddie was out on the streets, again but with nothing, not the nothing he was used to. There were plenty of times he started out with nothing but he had his hustle, his ability to get around and make money. Now, he had no will to even live, he wanted to die, he was going to stay by the dumpster and wait to die. After a few weeks, still having nothing but no closer to dying, he realized that dying could take a while, even his sense of humor was still with him and he laughed to himself about the idea that dying could take a while. He wasn't going to kill himself, after all, it wasn't easy to do, and he had already failed a couple times. His attacker was also unsuccessful in attempting to murder him, and he had the element of surprise, with a deadly weapon and from a distance of two feet.

He had nothing, emotionally, physically and spiritually. At the same time, he knew, if he was going to have to live the unknown length of time he would be waiting to die, he needed to have, at least, the minimal comforts in life. The few comforts he may have had in the past, which made surviving a little easier. He began to venture out from behind the dumpster. His view of himself now less than ever, he felt worse than the garbage, he was pond scum, a parasite and a loser beyond compare. He tried to think of something or someplace he could do something, anything to protect his wellbeing and give him a sense of security. He began to ask woman, if he could work for them, he told them he could cook, clean and whatever else they needed him to do, in exchange for room and board. He felt so little of himself, he even suggesting he be their slave. He figured it was all he was qualified to do. Only asking women, he felt, he would be perfect, just doing what they wanted, that he would make them happy, eliminate any arguments by simply doing what he was told to do. He felt he would be lucky if he was in that position. People that didn't know him already had thought he was weird, now were convinced.

Even those that knew him thought he was slipping away but he would explain the situation and would do it in a way that somehow made sense. His explanation was that he was garbage and he was acting accordingly. He had no phone and was unable to do anything at all, he thought, maybe, it was all meant to be, this was his fate.

If you were expecting a glorious ending, where Eddie reunites with his family and especially his children, that's not happening here. That is also the case for almost everyone else on these streets, they just fade away, dying on these streets from any number of ailments or sometimes, being killed by somebody, could be anyone, even police. When it comes to people on the streets, with nobody who loves and supports them, if they are killed, there is no investigation or a limited one at best. This happens because if nobody cares about them, why should the authorities. Nobody will take the time away from something people care about to waste time and find out what happened to them.

It was 2019, Eddie lost his wife thirteen years ago, April 2006. Since 2013, he has been homeless and he hasn't spoken to anyone in his family except his mom, who offered him no help. He has spent six years with no love and support at all. His family has spent six years of holidays, individual family member's celebrations, accomplishments and reunions without him. He had to go through several life altering events without them, where each time it would generate the same hurt that their absence would make him feel without having their love and support. It wasn't just the grief of the moment and the effects, going it alone, without his family there for him, was an additional cause for him to feel pain. It reiterated his place, as garbage, his directions to where the garbage goes, the dumpster. He realizes that he is dead to them and has been for some time. His dreams of seeing them or them showing up to help him are unlikely, as they have settled into life without him, as if he were dead.

Eddie walks now, without a phone, the burden of having any possession is too much for him to handle, he also feels safer having nothing now, especially around his peers. He thinks, "Is this freedom, after all possessions do end up owning the possessor?" He has given up, resigned to accept his fate, his home is the dumpster. He no longer has the resolve he once had, he is beaten, and he has nothing left, no reason to try anymore, and no reason to live.

He has this place he came to, that he fell in love with, a mere geographical location but to him the most beautiful place anyone can be, Sonoma County. It's here in Sonoma, ten years ago, where he came to find the ultimate, among these hills, where the most spectacular sunsets dazzle him, every night. The dark blue sky, reflecting the gigantic Pacific, a shade of blue he had never seen before. He remembers when he lived with Dina on Petaluma Hill, how for the first year, they felt like they were Adam with Eve in paradise. He looks out at the vineyard across the street, where they would walk, talk and make love and watch the sun set. Here there is no rainy season, it's rainbow season, hard to try and catch one. He looks around, as he always does, absorbing everything that is this life, this world, this whole experience, just stopping and looking here in Sonoma is hard not to do. This is Santa Rosa, nobody should have to tell you to smell the roses, and nobody had to tell Eddie. He recalls officiating fall soccer at Montgomery HS, how the harvest moon would rise over the goal, gigantic, on the night's horizon, dwarfing everything soccer. This is where he lived, Sonoma, from sunrise and the morning dew in the field, through the hot day until the dark blue in the sky turns pastel and the thin line of clouds, a pastel pink all meet the red sun on the horizon. Always spectacular sunsets, in Sonoma. Where else would anybody want to be? He did love it here and maybe he had found the ultimate here.

Maybe giving into temptation when you have been given the ultimate is punishable, payable to the keeper of darkness and he is paying. Does the punishment fit the crime? Did he hurt anybody, while giving in to temptation, after all he did loss paradise? None the less, this is where he is and this is where he will stay. He walks and feels the wind in his face, it makes his cheek flutter, at the spot of the entry wound from the attack on the greyhound, reminding him of the vicious attack. He is also constantly clearing his throat, since then, a permanent condition, turrets or PTSD.

This life is hard for everybody, everybody hurts, even those that live in big houses and have a lot of money. The directions Eddie got were worse than any, they leave you where there are no comforts, no love and no support, no security and a wellbeing that is constantly at stake. Sure, everybody hurts and endures some pain and suffering but they have food, shelter and their wellbeing is secured.

In his head plays one last song, for now, he hears, 'Gimmie Shelter" "Oh, a storm is threat'ning', my very life today, If I don't get some shelter, Oh yeah, I'm gonna fade away. War, children, it's just a shot away, It's just a shot away. War, children, it's just a shot away. It's just a shot away, Ooh, see the fire is sweepin', our very street today. Burns like a red coal carpet, mad bull lost its way, war, children, it's just a shot away. It's just a shot away. War, children, it's just a shot away, It's just a shot away. Rape, murder! It's just a shot away, it's just a shot away. Rape, murder yeah! It's just a shot away. It's just a shot away. Rape, murder! It's just a shot away. It's just a shot away yea. The floods is threat, my very life today. Gimme, gimme shelter or I'm gonna fade away
War, children, it's just a shot away. It's just a shot away. I tell you love, sister, it's just a kiss away. It's just a kiss away. It's just a kiss away. It's just a kiss away. It's just a kiss away. Kiss away, kiss away."

Although Eddie retreats to his home, now, what he thinks must be the dumpster, where he will wait for his death. Like so many others out on these streets, once they have surrendered to their fate, accepted the destination their directions have led them to, they will either be killed, die from a disease, disappear or fade away. With his belongings, all of them, packed in his back pack, a homeless person's ball and chain, he throws up his left arm, bringing the back pack higher on his back and he clicks it in to secure it. Paining his back and shoulders, he disappears into the waste management area, aka, the dumpster. Where there is no mattress, only cardboard on concrete, where any season, it hurts.

He knows, this will not do, he knows, he has to tell his daughter how much she is loved by him and was by her mom, how much they wanted her and had planned for her. He knows his son still has much to learn, that he can teach him. He knows he has gained more wisdom than he could have imagined through experiences he wants to soon forget. He knows, he has to try again and that he still has love to give. He knows he can do anything but he has almost forgotten, he wrote a book, he needs to fulfil his obligation to the publisher, perhaps, he hasn't given up yet.

He has written a book and he thinks that maybe there is a chance his book will reach some people. He thinks it can only be good, to educate society about the most misunderstood segment of its population, the homeless. That they will reconsider the way they themselves and society view the homeless. That society will think about the directions they give to others and consider more, where the directions they give will have them end up. He wants people to know that we are all not in control of where we end up and that others who have made huge decisions that affected us in a very negative way and have directed us to a place we didn't want to be. It's those people, the victimizers, which want you to believe everything is in your own control. Who owns the choices that we didn't get to make? What if a choice is to stand up for what is right and doing so hurts us?

People should know that bad things happen to good people. That there are people who have unconditional love for one another, who display random acts of kindness for strangers, who are down and out, are in a situation where their wellbeing is not secured, as it is they who are homeless. People should know that their labels are wrong and unfairly define individuals like this, making their lives much more difficult than they already are and impossible to get out of their situation. People should know that they are not all thieves, drug attics and bad people. People should know that the answer is simple and the answer is love, people on the streets need love to find their hearts and where their home is. Everywhere, anytime, no matter what, the answer is love.

He hopes that his family and friends, mostly his children will read it and realize how much love he has to give and wants to share with them. How he wishes he could find the home he has in his heart, with them, his children. A beautiful place in his heart, where he is with his children and someday his grandchildren. A place in his heart where he can share his love for them, have moments with them, to help them, to lend his many experiences, to use his infinite wisdom to give them directions that keep them away from the dumpster. "Fast Eddie" wants, to direct them to a beautiful home, on Happy Street, a home sweet home in their hearts, that is filled with peace and love.

The end

Made in the USA
Columbia, SC
05 July 2019